The Last Adventure of Napoleon Sunshine

ALSO BY PASCAL RUTER

A Friend in the Dark

The Last Adventure of Napoleon Sunshine

Pascal Ruter

Translated by Simon Pare

Little, Brown

LITTLE, BROWN

First published in France in 2017 by Éditions Jean-Claude Lattès/
Didier Jeunesse as *Barracuda For Ever*
First published in Great Britain in 2019 by Little, Brown

1 3 5 7 9 10 8 6 4 2

A CIP catalogue record for this book
is available from the British Library.

ISBN: 978-1-4087-1026-5

Typeset in Garamond by M Rules
Printed and bound in Great Britain by
Clays Ltd, Elcograf S.p.A.

Papers used by Little, Brown are from well-managed forests
and other responsible sources.

MIX
Paper from
responsible sources
FSC® C104740

Little, Brown
An imprint of
Little, Brown Book Group
Carmelite House
50 Victoria Embankment
London EC4Y 0DZ

An Hachette UK Company
www.hachette.co.uk

www.littlebrown.co.uk

For Michèle Moreau, without whom these pages would never have become a novel.

With my warmest thanks.

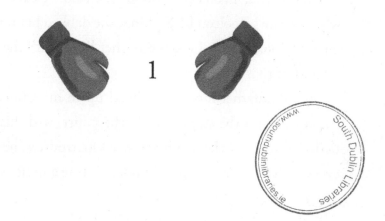

1

At the age of eighty-five my grandfather Napoleon decided he needed to try something new. He took my grandmother Josephine to court. She never had been able to resist him and she went along with his wishes this time too. Their divorce came through on the first day of autumn.

'I want to start a new life,' he'd told the presiding judge.

'And you're entitled to do so,' the judge ruled.

My parents and I had accompanied them to the law courts. My father was hoping that Napoleon would chicken out at the last minute, but I knew he wouldn't: my grandfather never changed his mind. Whatever he said usually went, despite what we all said.

My grandmother Josephine cried throughout. I held her

by the arm and passed her tissues that were sodden with tears in a few seconds.

'Thank you, Leonard darling,' she said. 'I can't believe what a brute Napoleon is!' Sighing, she dabbed her nose, and an affectionate smile flickered on her lips. 'If it's the brute's own idea, that is.'

My grandfather more than lived up to his name. As he stood there on the steps outside the court, with his hands thrust into the pockets of his new white trousers, he looked every inch the proud empire-builder casting a smug, satisfied eye over his newly conquered realm.

I admired him. I believed that life held many secrets and my grandfather knew them all.

The early autumn air was mild and damp. Josephine shivered and turned up the collar of her coat.

'Let's celebrate!' Napoleon declared.

Dad and Mum disagreed with this suggestion and Josephine was even more strongly against it, so we simply headed towards the metro.

Outside the station was an ice-cream stand.

'Fancy a vanilla ice cream?' Napoleon asked me. He held out a bank note to the young vendor. 'Two ice creams – one for me and one for my friend here. Whipped cream? Why not. We'll have some whipped cream, won't we, pal?'

He winked at me. I nodded back. Mum shrugged. Dad stared straight ahead, his eyes blank.

'Of course my pal wants whipped cream!'

He'd always called me 'pal'. I didn't really know when it had caught on, but I liked to think that everyone called each another 'pal' in the gyms and rings where he used to box.

'Pal' felt like someone completely different from Leonard. Leonard Sunshine. I was ten. The world still seemed incomprehensible, mysterious and a little hostile, and I often felt an overpowering sense that my puny physique wouldn't get me very far in the world. Napoleon reassured me by saying that a boxer didn't need to be well built and that most champions had developed successful careers on the strength of their class and talent. I wasn't a boxer, though – I was the invisible boy.

I'd made my entrance into this world one stormy evening. The bulbs in the operating theatre had blown and so my very first cries in this world were delivered in darkness. Little Sunshine had arrived in the dark, and the intervening ten years hadn't entirely dispelled that darkness.

'Like it, pal?' Napoleon asked me.

'It's delicious!' I replied. 'Thank you.'

My grandma had calmed down a bit by now. Our eyes met and she smiled.

'Enjoy it,' she whispered.

The vendor held out the change to Napoleon, who asked him, 'How old are you?'

'Twenty-three, *monsieur*. Why?'

'No reason, I just wanted to know. Keep the change. Go on, I'm serious. We're celebrating!'

'Whatever next!' my grandma said under her breath.

None of us talked on the train back, which was full of people heading home from work. My grandma had recovered some of her confidence. She'd reapplied her lipstick and I'd snuggled up to her, as if sensing that we would soon be separated. She was resting her forehead against the window, watching the world pass by. Sadness lent her a kind of beautiful dignity. She cast the occasional glance at the man with whom she had shared her life. I wondered what thoughts lay behind the fleeting smile that broke through her sadness every so often. I told myself that she was capable of understanding and enduring anything.

My grandfather had a white ice-cream moustache. He'd put his feet up on the seat opposite and started to whistle.

'What a wonderful day it's been!' he exclaimed.

'Exactly the word I'd have chosen,' my grandma muttered.

2

The following week, all of us, Napoleon included, accompanied Josephine from our home just outside Paris to the Gare de Lyon. She'd decided to return to her birthplace close to Aix-en-Provence in the south of France where a small house, vacated by her niece, awaited her. You had to look on the bright side, she said. She'd catch up with old friends and tread the familiar paths of her youth, and above all there'd be plenty of warmth and light.

'I'll be warmer than you!'

As if to confirm her words, a fine drizzle began to fall.

We waited for the train among stacks of suitcases. My grandfather paced up and down the platform as if afraid the train would never arrive.

'You will come and see me, Leonard poppet?' my grandma asked.

My mother answered on my behalf. 'Of course we will. Often. It really isn't very far.'

'And you'll come and see us too,' my father added.

'If Napoleon calls me I'll come. Tell him that. I know that brute better than anyone else, and I'm perfectly aware of what ...' She stopped and seemed to reflect for a few seconds before continuing, 'Oh, actually, forget it. Don't tell him anything. He'll beg me himself once he's stewed for long enough. Stewed like a leg of mutton ...'

Approaching us with short strides, my grandfather interrupted her. 'The train's pulling in. Make sure you're ready! You mustn't miss it!'

'You really do have a knack for saying the right things, don't you?' my father said.

Grabbing the largest suitcase, Napoleon turned to my grandma Josephine and said softly, 'I got you a first-class ticket.'

'How sweet of you!' she said with a forced smile.

We helped her to her seat. Napoleon and my father wedged her suitcases into every available nook and cranny.

I overheard my grandfather whispering to another passenger, 'Keep an eye on her. She may not look it, but she's actually quite fragile.'

'What did you say to that lady?' my grandmother asked.

'Nothing, nothing. I was telling her that the trains are always delayed.'

We all got out onto the platform. The announcer

informed us that the train for Aix-en-Provence was ready to depart. Josephine put on her best smile again at the window, as if she were only going on holiday.

The train slid past us, and we each gave her a little wave. Then the red taillights of the rearmost carriage disappeared into the mist and it was over. There was an announcement for another train. More travellers flooded onto the platform.

'Let's have a drink!' Napoleon said. 'This one's on me.'

He found us a booth in a busy café filled with tourists and we crammed ourselves into it. He told us of his many projects.

'First, I'm going to redo the house,' he said. 'Hang new wallpaper, give it a fresh lick of paint, mend a few things here and there. A facelift, you know.'

'I'll get some builders in for you,' my father said.

'No builders. I'm going to do everything myself. My pal here will give me a hand.' He accompanied his words with a punch to my shoulder.

'That probably isn't very wise,' my mother said. 'You should listen to your son.'

My father nodded and added, 'That's right, Dad. Think this through. It might be easier to have a builder take care of it. He can do the bulk of the work.'

'Oh yeah,' my grandfather cried, 'and I'll just sit around, shall I? No way! I'm going to do it all myself. I didn't ask for your opinion. If you can't support me and my plans then

I don't want to hear it. I'll be just fine on my own – I'll be even better when I put in a gym.'

'A gym?' my father exclaimed.

'Good idea, don't you think?'

My father sighed and exchanged glances with my mother before clearing his throat, 'Honestly, Dad, if you want my thoughts on this—'

'Save your breath,' Napoleon cut him off, sucking up Coke through his straw. 'I'm fully aware of what you think of all this.'

Nope, they didn't approve – particularly my father. You don't get divorced at eighty-five, going on eighty-six. You don't add to your house at that age and you *do* accept help with renovating and redecorating. In fact, you don't redecorate at all at that age. You wait. You wait for the end to come.

'You know,' Napoleon went on, 'I couldn't care less what you make of all this. I don't need your permission. Got that?'

My father started to go red. His face creased up as if someone had flicked a switch, but my mother's hand came to rest on his forearm, dousing his anger.

'I think so, yes.'

Napoleon winked, came close and said to me, 'Do you think I've made myself sufficiently clear, pal?'

I nodded.

Sometimes I felt as if we had our own private language, and we used it whenever we had a secret to share. Often when adults were around, my grandfather liked to whisper a remark, share some confidence with me in a straightforward manner, unlike a lot of other grown-ups who went round in circles without really getting to the point. My grandfather's direct way was learned during his life as a whirlwind fighter in the boxing ring; it was what enabled him to communicate effortlessly with boxers from other countries, to rig bouts and pull the wool over everyone's eyes – trainers, promoters and journalists.

'What did he say?' my father asked.

'Nothing,' I replied. 'He says it's very kind of you to worry about him.'

We left the station. Outside, an unbroken line of taxis were waiting for passengers.

'Hey!' my grandfather shouted at one driver. 'Are you free?'

'Yep, I'm free.'

'Good,' said Napoleon, 'because so am I.' He guffawed at his own joke.

3

Napoleon had already had two lives and, like a cat, he probably had a few more in reserve, even at his age. During his first career he'd fought in boxing rings and been front-page news all over the world. He'd tasted the shady fame of championship bouts, blizzards of flashbulbs, the short-lived joy of victory and the infinite solitude of the changing room after a defeat. Then, one day, he'd called time on his career for reasons unknown to us.

He'd reinvented himself as a taxi driver – or a *cab driver*, as he used to call it in a phoney American accent. He'd switch on his sign when he picked me up from school, and the letters 'T', 'A' and 'I' would light up in the dark winter nights, while the 'X' refused to come on. He would open the back door of his Peugeot 404 and in a solemn voice ask, 'Where would the young gentleman like to go today?'

Grandpa also picked up passengers more or less when he felt like it, and I can only imagine what they thought of his unconventional ways.

But that Friday, a week after Josephine's departure, he announced, 'I'm taking you somewhere.'

'Bowling?'

'No, not bowling? You'll find out soon enough.'

Napoleon explained that after much deliberation he had decided that he should begin the next phase of his life with a significant event.

'A happy event! One full of sunshine,' he exclaimed, ignoring a Give Way sign.

'OK, but you're on the wrong side of the road, Grandpa.'

'Never mind,' he answered. 'They drive on the wrong side of the road in England.'

'But this isn't England!'

'Why's everyone honking at me?'

'Which year did you pass your driving test, Grandpa?'

'First, you're not allowed to call me that from now on. And second – what test?'

The sun was starting to sink in the sky.

Every time we came to a junction and he needed to slam on the brakes, he would automatically reach over to stop me from flying head first through the windscreen, as the car still had old, slack seatbelts. We drove for half an hour before turning off the road onto a dirt track.

'It's here. Or at least I think it is.'

I read the letters on the sign above the entrance. 'S.P.A.'

'Good – you know three letters of the alphabet. That's quite enough to be getting on with. Come on, *vamos*. Let's go.'

'The Society for the Protection of Animals? You want to adopt a dog?' I asked as we walked along the aisles between rows of kennels.

'No . . . as you can see, I'm looking for a secretary! You do come out with some stupid questions sometimes.'

A series of rasping barks and high-pitched yapping emerged from the cages. They seemed to contain every breed of dog under the sun, with coats of every kind – long, fine, short, thick, straight and curly. Most of them lay at the backs of their cages with downcast expressions on their faces, but they would wag their tails excitedly whenever a visitor passed.

Some of the dogs had mange and scratched desperately at their scabs; some had runny eyes and others spun in circles, chasing their tails. Here was a sturdy spaniel, there a Beauceron; in one cage was a fiery-tempered Jack Russell, in the next a placid Labrador, an elegant collie or a graceful, noble-looking greyhound. We were spoilt for choice, and that was a problem.

'It isn't easy to choose,' Napoleon said, 'and we can't take them all. We can't possibly draw lots . . . '

A woman came over to meet us. She must have caught wind of my grandfather's indecision as she said, 'It depends what you want the dog for.'

'That's the trouble – we don't know,' Napoleon replied.

12

'What a silly thing to say! We simply want a dog we can treat like a dog, full stop.' Pointing to a cage with no sign attached to the bars, he said, 'What's that one there?'

'That one?' the woman said. 'A wire fox terrier, I think.'

The dog looked at us through one milky eye, briefly raised its muzzle and then, with a long sigh, laid it between its parallel paws again.

'Are you sure?' Napoleon asked.

'Not really. A setter? Probably. Maybe. Hold on a second and I'll check.' The woman got the papers she was carrying in a muddle, and they started flying about in all directions. 'We just have so many dogs . . .'

'Oh, never mind the breed. We don't care about the breed anyway, do we, pal?'

'Er . . . no, we don't care.'

'How old is he?'

The lady adopted a self-confident and professional air. 'Um . . . about a year. No, two. Yes, that's right.' Her face dissolved into an embarrassed smile. 'Actually, he may be younger. Or a lot older.' She leafed through her remaining papers, and this time she sent the whole lot sailing across the enclosure.

'OK, forget it!' said Napoleon. 'We don't care how old he is either. So how long does a dog like this live for?'

'They're very resilient. Just under twenty years,' the woman answered. 'You look worried. Is that a problem?'

'Of course it's a problem!' Napoleon cried.

'Ah, I see. I think I understand ...'

'Yes,' said Napoleon. 'That's the trouble with animals – they always die before you do and that breaks your heart!'

'How funny,' said Napoleon. 'There were only two of us when we arrived, and now there are three of us leaving.'

We exchanged smiles. I wanted to talk to the dog, but it seemed faintly ridiculous so I didn't dare.

Napoleon took from his pocket a brand-new lead that unwound like a snake. It still had its price tag.

'You thought of everything, Gran— ... I mean, Napoleon.'

'Everything. Even that – look!'

The boot of the Peugeot 404 was filled to bursting with sacks of dog biscuits. Napoleon opened the back door of the car and solemnly announced, 'The start of a new life! Where would the young gentleman like to go next?'

The animal jumped onto the back seat, gave it a sniff and, finding it to his liking, made himself comfortable.

The defective taxi meter was stuck on '0000', and I truly believed this signalled the start of something.

'It's true,' said Napoleon, putting the car into first gear, 'there's no need to have a specific breed of dog. All you need is a dog. A dog-like dog!'

Then there was the matter of naming the dog. Buster, Rin Tin Tin, Rex: none of those really caught our fancy. At a red light the two of us looked round, and the animal raised two soft, enquiring eyes.

'You,' said my grandfather, 'deserve to be called some-thing unique. Something new. Out with all those old names. That's right – you need a distinctive name. End of story.'

'End of!' I cried. 'That's a good name.'

'All right then, Endov it is.' Looking at the dog, my grand-father said, 'So, Endov, are you happy to have a name at last?'

'Woof!'

'He seems to like it!' I said. 'It's green – you can go.'

'A fine name,' my grandfather said as he drove off. 'For a dog, in any case. It's original. Distinguished. Classy, you know. No one else will have it. I can tell you two are going to get on very well.'

When we reached Napoleon's house we took the sacks of dog biscuits out of his car and stuffed them into cupboards.

'Good work,' said Napoleon. 'Now, I've got some-thing for you.'

He opened a drawer and pulled out a bulging canvas bag.

'Don't worry, it isn't dog biscuits. Open it.' His eyes shone mischievously.

Marbles. Hundreds of marbles. Old marbles. Some made of clay, others of glass. Aggies, taws, ducks ... Napoleon's childhood in a bag.

'They're not the newest,' he said. 'It took me years to win them all. You'll get more use out of them than I will. I don't have many friends left to play marbles with, you see. Grandfathers usually pass on their stamp collections, but stamps bored me to death. For one thing, I didn't receive many letters. Then again, I didn't bust a gut to send any either.'

My legs felt as if they were made of jelly, my heart was racing and my jaw was locked tight.

'You aren't going to start blubbing, are you?' he scolded.

4

Endov joined our family and was introduced to my parents the following day. Napoleon brought him to the house. He was an easy-going dog, docile, gentle but easily excited.

All my father could say was, 'What breed is it?'

'He's a dog,' Napoleon replied. 'Nothing more and nothing less. I don't know why, but I was sure you'd ask that.'

'No need to get all worked up,' my father snorted. 'It was only a question. Often you say, "It's a Poodle" or "a Labrador" or "a Poi—"'

'Not in this case, though. Let's just say, "It's a dog". A dog crossed with a dog,' Napoleon said.

'OK, OK. Don't get annoyed about it.'

'I'm not. Endov's his name. And you know what, I *am* getting annoyed about it. Annoyed by your constant need to categorise everything,' Napoleon continued. 'Even as a kid you categorised everything. Remember your stamps? You always did like to put people – and dogs – into boxes, just to make sure they stay put, like in—'

My father interrupted, 'Well, can you at least tell me why you've gone and got a dog now? Now that—'

'Now that what?'

'Now . . . nothing.'

Napoleon waved his arms, making exaggerated gestures, as he explained that he'd always longed to own a dog. When he was a boy they'd lived in a tiny flat in Belleville, and later, once he became a boxer, there was no point in even entertaining the idea – which dog, even one as accommodating and pleasant as Endov, would have put up with the rootless life of a boxer?

'Also, your mother was allergic to dog hair. Just my luck! But now I'm determined to look after him to the bitter end.'

My father raised a quizzical eyebrow.

'*His* bitter end,' Napoleon added with a shrug.

My mother had taken out her pencils and sketchbook, open at a blank page, as all of this was going on. Endov seemed to take an interest in what she was doing and adopted a regal pose. He was born to be immortalised in my mother's sketchbook.

I liked to watch her work. She drew everything she saw around her, becoming so utterly absorbed by her chosen subject that nothing else seemed to exist. She spoke little, as if she'd only a limited stock of words, but she'd draw all the things she couldn't say. Three quick lines, and people came to life on the page. Quick as a flash, her pencil would capture the glint in a person's eye or a tiny, seemingly trivial gesture that revealed a great deal about someone's character. Drawers were filled with these little spontaneous sketches. Bound together in albums, they would sometimes tell rambling yet quite poetic stories. She would often visit libraries and schools to share them.

My father examined the animal from all sides and, after consulting an encyclopaedia, announced that it was a mix of fox terrier, greyhound, spaniel and Maltese. It was a patchwork dog. Its long fluffy tail was particularly puzzling; it looked as if it had been added to Endov's body as an afterthought. While we were identifying and classifying Endov, I put my hand in my pocket, into which I had transferred a few of my favourite marbles, and ran my fingers over them. I was excited about my new present.

'By the way,' said Napoleon, turning to my father, 'now that things have settled down a bit, I've got a favour to ask.'

He removed a bundle of typewritten sheets of paper from a large envelope.

'See, the judge wrote to me. Would you mind reading it aloud? I would read it myself, but I left my glasses at home.'

My father took the document and started to skim through it. 'Let's have a look at this . . . "Grounds for divorce: new lease of life." Good grief, Dad, you've got a nerve.'

Napoleon smiled proudly, and Endov seemed to shoot him an admiring glance.

'So, summing up, this states that you both agreed and there were no conflicts or objections.'

'Exactly,' said Napoleon. 'Everyone was happy, and it all went smoothly.'

'For you, maybe,' my father said. 'I'm not quite so sure about Josephine . . .'

'Tut-tut! How would you know? Anyway, what about the rest of the letter?'

'It all seems pretty standard. Oh, hang on, what's this . . .?'

'What's what?' Napoleon demanded.

My father's eyes moved to the bottom of the last page. 'Know what the judge added in pencil? "Best of luck!"'

'Nice chap, that judge,' my grandfather said. 'I felt we really bonded. In fact, I almost suggested we go for a beer afterwards.' Napoleon grabbed the document from my father's hands. 'I'm going to frame this and hang it in my bathroom to commemorate the beginning of my new life.' He thrust the ream of paper under my nose. 'See this, pal? It'll make a fine certificate. I'm going to put it up next to my picture of Rocky!'

He smiled. His blue eyes sparkled under his mop of white hair, a few strands of which would occasionally fall over his face. I admired his attitude. I appreciated the youthful glint in his eye, surrounded by a web of fine wrinkles. His hands were always clenched into fists, even if he had no reason to be annoyed.

'If you're happy, that's fantastic,' my father said. 'I know you don't like us sticking our noses into your business and that you don't care about my opinion, but I think you've been too hard on Mum. There, I've said it.'

'You're right,' said Napoleon, only to wipe the look of satisfaction off my father's face by adding, 'on two counts: I don't like people sticking their noses into my business and I don't give two hoots about your opinion.'

Napoleon turned to me and asked, 'Don't you think he's an idiot?'

I just smiled.

'What did he say, Leonard?' my father enquired.

'Oh, nothing,' I replied. 'Only that it's very kind of you to worry about him. He's grateful.' I felt for the marbles still in my pocket.

A smile lit up my father's face, instantly filling me with sorrow. My mother put an arm around his shoulders.

'It's absolutely true,' my grandfather grumbled.

The next day at school I met Alexandre Rawcziik for the first time. Double 'I', as he immediately pointed out. He guarded his two 'I's as jealously as I did Napoleon's marbles, keeping them hidden in my schoolbag. He wore a strange cap made of fur, leather, velvet and the odd feather or two, which he hung up carefully on a coat peg in the corridor, as if it were a helmet. I was mesmerised by it.

Alexandre came across as a little shy and slightly sad

and lonely, which immediately made him stand out from the other kids in my class, and made me feel sympathetic towards him. I was surprised to find that within a few hours I considered him my best friend. Was it my happiness at having finally found a classmate who was like me and with whom I could share everything? Was it the magic effect of Napoleon's marbles that was making my life interesting? It was a mystery to me. Whatever it was, intoxicated by a new sense of invincibility, I had no second thoughts about suggesting a game of marbles to Alexandre. Convinced that I could multiply the treasure Napoleon had entrusted to me, I staked his marbles on the game.

One by one I watched them disappear into my new friend's pockets. I kept pulling fresh ones from the old bag in the unwavering belief that I'd be able to win them back: my luck was bound to change. It didn't happen, though. Some black magic was making the marbles deviate from their path, causing them to swerve at the last moment and miss their target.

Alexandre took his winnings, without so much as a glance at me. The marbles rattled together as they piled up in his pocket. I told myself that I ought to stop or I'd lose everything, but each time, despite these thoughts, my hand dipped into my pocket and I threw a new marble into the game. He was devilishly skilful, and his throws were as accurate as sniper fire.

The least attractive marbles vanished first, then the

shiniest ones, and soon the most precious ones were gone. I'd lost all my riches in a single day.

'Game over,' I said. 'I don't have any left.'

Strangely, I didn't hold it against Alexandre. I'd squandered something sacred, and I had only myself to blame.

I went home with a bag as empty as my heart, and a lump in my throat from sobbing. What on earth had got into me? Why did I have to see it through to the bitter end? It was too late now, though.

5

The day after the tragedy of the marbles, my grandfather announced, 'I name you my aide-de-camp, pal. I appoint Leonard Sunshine my aide-de-camp. There, it's official.'

'At your command, your imperial highness!' I said, standing to attention like a soldier.

'We're going to attack all the burnt-out light bulbs to give us a brighter view of the future. All right, pal?'

'You're on.'

I held a stool onto which he clambered to unscrew a bulb.

'Are you sure you switched off the power, Grandpa?'

'Don't you worry, pal. And don't call me Grandpa.'

'OK, Grandpa. I'm not worried, I just don't want you ending up like Claude François.' Claude François was a famous pop star in the sixties, and Grandpa was a fan of his songs.

'Poor old Cloclo. I feel a pang of sadness every time I think of him. Fiddling with a light fitting while in the shower . . . Ha ha ha!' He was laughing so hard that he could barely keep his balance on the stool. 'OK, let's get down to business. Pass me the new bulb.'

There was a shower of sparks around his hand, and the room went dark.

'Ouch! Shit!' he said, jumping off the stool. 'I must have forgotten something. I don't get it, though. I did all the electrics in this house myself – I thought I'd switched everything off. Your grandmother must have got someone to change the wiring, and now look what's happened. Always beware of women.'

He dug out a candle from somewhere and lit it.

'And then there was light!' he declared proudly.

Endov was greatly amused by these goings-on. He sat there wagging his tail and panting. He seemed to be waiting expectantly for the next bit of entertainment.

'Hey, pal?'

'Yes.'

'Nice and cosy here with just the two of us, isn't it?' he said, dropping down on the old sofa.

'The *three* of us!' I corrected him, stroking Endov.

It occurred to me that we looked like burglars in the dark house.

'I wonder if he's a good guard dog,' Napoleon said.

Endov rolled over onto his back and stuck out his belly to be scratched.

'Come and sit over here,' my grandfather said, patting the sofa next to him. I've got something to tell you.'

His voice was quiet, and it wavered slightly. For a split second I felt incredibly worried. My grandmother Josephine's absence filled the room, and I was sure that Napoleon could feel it too.

'My old pal,' he sighed, 'some people are still with us even when we can no longer see them.'

In spite of the circumstances, he was very relaxed. I noticed that his gnarled hands were spread over his knees. The candle flickered across the room.

'Blimey, that candle is really burning down quickly! It's rather beautiful, isn't it,' my grandfather whispered, then shook himself, as if surprised by his own remark. 'OK, our melancholy moment is over. Enough philosophising. Time for an arm-wrestle!'

We played this game from time to time. We took up positions opposite each other. Our hands met, palm to palm. Our muscles strained. Our arms pivoted first to the right, then to the left. Our faces twisted into pirate-like grimaces. He pretended to grit his teeth and suffer; I was going to beat him this time. Yet just as victory was within my grasp and the back of his hand was hovering half an inch above the table top, he cracked a grin, started to whistle and examine the nails of his other hand and, effortlessly, delicately, turned the tables on me. My hand traced a semicircle and slammed down on the other side of the table.

Just then there was a knock on the front door.

'Are you expecting someone?' I asked.

'No. Go and get the door. I'm going to try to find this fuse. We don't get a minute's peace.'

There were two men at the door, wearing identical suits and carrying identical briefcases.

'Is anyone else at home?' one of the callers enquired.

The lights came back on, and my grandfather appeared behind me. To my great surprise he let them into the house without checking their credentials and invited them to take a seat at the table. I noticed that his fists were clenched again.

'We're going to have a fine time, pal. They won't last three rounds,' Napoleon said.

The two men took some brochures and catalogues from their briefcases. Grandfather looked curious.

'This here,' one of the salesmen said, 'this item you see here, is a rail that we can install along the banister to enable you to get up the stairs without tiring yourself out . . . Think of it as a small, private chair-lift. The best on the market.'

'Not bad. And what's that?'

'An acoustic aid for people with reduced hearing.'

'A what?' Napoleon said, cupping his hand to his ear.

'An acoustic aid for—'

'A moose-tick aid, did you say? No need for that – no moose or ticks around here. We do get some pains in the neck, though.'

The two men glanced at each other, then both squeezed out a smile.

'And what's this?' my grandfather asked, jabbing his finger at a different picture.

'Magnifying glasses for people with impaired vision.'

'How interesting. Mind you, with all the ugly faces we get around here ... And this? That's odd – it looks like something for a toddler. A scooter.'

'It's the latest rolling walker. Titanium and carbon. Fitted with disc brakes. For people with reduced mobility. I'm guessing you have planned for the future?'

'Absolutely. It's a stroke of luck that you've dropped by. I think about the future all the time.'

The two door-to-door salesmen had satisfied smiles on their faces.

Napoleon winked at me as they were looking down at their catalogue.

The touchpaper had been lit, and all I could do now was watch and wait for the powder keg to blow sky-high. Wait quietly, as you would at a fireworks display.

'Good, let's talk about the future,' one of the two men said. 'Let's talk about it seriously.'

'I'm going to talk to *you* about *your* future,' replied Napoleon, as he sat there, with crossed arms and eyes as keen as darts. 'And I'm going to do it seriously.'

The salesmen glanced at me. They were trapped. I shrugged.

'Your immediate future, you wretched gits, is to stop hassling us. Your short- to medium-term future, on the other hand, will be a punch in the face. Could you please enlighten me as to the kind of people all this crap is aimed at?'

'Um, I don't know ... the elderly, I guess.'

'Old people, you mean?' Grandpa asked, raising one eyebrow. 'Spit it out now!'

'Um, yes, that's right ... those kinds of people.'

Napoleon was tapping his foot mechanically on the floor and he turned to me. 'Because I suppose you can see an *old person* in this house? Can't you, pal?'

'No,' I said, twisting on my chair as if to scour the room for signs of one. 'No one of that description here. Even Endov is a whippersnapper.'

'Woof!'

The two featherweights stammered something. They didn't dare challenge my grandfather any further. He seemed to loom over them, filling the room from floor to ceiling. He slammed his hand down hard on the table, which almost split it in two. The catalogues leaped into the air.

'Blistering barnacles, do you see an old person in this room? Yes or no? Damn you. It's a very simple question! Even idiots like you should know the right answer if you want to get out of here unharmed.'

His arm shot out, sending the catalogues sailing into the wall.

'No, we don't see any old people here ... We got the

wrong address. No old people here at all. We should prob-ably be going.'

We heard their car drive off at full speed.

'Shit,' said my grandfather. 'Those vultures will kill me before my time. Come on, pal, I need to work that out of my system.' He stood up.

I knew exactly what he meant, so he and I put on gloves and got into position opposite each other.

'OK, pal. Now box. *Box!* Come on – let's see you move those legs.'

Napoleon was so thin and his limbs so slender that you could barely see him from side on. From the front, though, he looked as tall as a mountain.

'Keep your guard up! And watch my legs.'

With his fists raised in front of his face and his torso bent forward, he really did resemble the boxer he'd once been. He looked indestructible in this pose, ready to fight all challengers.

He'd disputed the world light heavyweight title in 1952, losing narrowly on points. To a boxer who had, perhaps unimaginatively, called himself Rocky. I knew that bout off by heart – his final fight, which had made headlines all over the world, had been the high point of his boxing career and had also spelled the end of it. He'd hung up his gloves immediately after the defeat. I'd never been bold enough to ask him about the fateful match, but that day, without quite knowing why, I asked him, 'What stopped you winning that fight? Do you know?'

At this point he was concentrating so hard that he didn't appear to have heard my question and long seconds trailed away before he eventually put down his boxing gloves and said, 'Nothing. Nothing stopped me – other than a crooked referee.'

He wiped his hands on a little white towel, and I felt keenly that this was a sign that I shouldn't ask any more questions.

'And don't believe for a second what the papers said,' he continued as if he could read my mind. 'All rubbish! A pack of lies!' He put out dog food for Endov, who buried his face deep in his bowl and started to chomp away.

'Dogs have such huge appetites! Unbelievable, isn't it?' He glanced up at me, with a far-off look in his eye. The candle on the table was guttering. My grandfather blew out the flame.

'Why did you give up after that fight?' I asked. 'That's what I don't understand. Why didn't you ask for an immediate rematch?'

'Come and have a look.'

He led me to the toilet, which was a real shrine to boxing – a pristine, intact slice of the past. On the wall were a number of photos of various fights. In these photos Napoleon's slender, muscular legs were poking out of an oversized pair of white satin shorts. He clenched his jaw as he dealt out uppercuts, planted a straight right or skilfully absorbed his opponent's hook in defence. Still unbeaten, never knocked out.

31

'Listen, pal.'

I looked up at him.

'Can you hear the crowd? Can you hear them baying? And the thud of punches landing?'

All I could hear was the gurgle of the leaking toilet cistern, but I nodded anyway.

Napoleon was lost in contemplation while standing in front of the photos. 'I haven't changed a bit, have I, pal? Time hasn't left a mark on me.'

'No, Grandpa. You haven't changed a bit. In fact, you'll never change. That's right, isn't it? You won't ever change?'

'Never. I promise.'

Napoleon planted himself in front of the portrait of Rocky. His eyes narrowed. His shoulders quivered.

Square-jawed, tight-lipped, his shoulders glistening with sweat. Raised fists shadowing his cheeks. Rocky, the great Rocky – Napoleon's final opponent.

Napoleon sighed. 'A rematch with Rocky? That thief really did me over – he died soon after of some stupid disease, can't remember what. I swear I sometimes hear him sniggering. That bastard really stitched me up!'

Napoleon reckoned we'd done enough work for one day. He announced that he had a phone call to make.

'To the Wet Blanket,' he announced.

6

'Wet Blanket' was my father. For many years I didn't understand what this mysterious phrase meant. I guessed it must
be a special term of endearment. However, when I was old
enough to grasp its meaning, I couldn't help feeling a pang
of unease every time my grandfather used it. He sometimes
said it to my father's face and I could obviously understand
how upset it made my father.

'Hi, is that you? I'm taking your son bowling.' He shot
me a wink. 'When will we be back? Haven't a clue. What
kind of question is that? You know full well I've never owned
a watch. The one you gave me? I lost it. Or sold it, I can't
remember. And see, you know when bowling starts, but
not where it might take you. No, that's true – you wouldn't
know. His homework? Yeah, we've done it.'

My grandfather placed his hand over the receiver and

whispered to me, 'He's chewing my ear off. Get ready, we'll be off in a minute.'

He then pressed the telephone back to his ear. 'The grammar test – yeah, of course. Dictation too – who do you take me for? Everything's fine.'

By now I had got out the bowling ball and our shoes. Napoleon hung up.

'See that, pal? I lied to Wet Blanket. He's obsessed with homework. It's a good thing you don't take after him.'

My heart tightened. I merely smiled at him. We don't always take after the people we most admire.

Napoleon put on his black leather jacket and we left the house, hiding the keys under the mat. He opened the door of the Peugeot 404 for me.

'If the young gentleman would care to step inside.'

Grandpa had his own bowling ball. It was black, shiny and very heavy and it was engraved with the words 'Born to Win'. This same phrase had been embroidered in white thread on his boxing gloves. He thought it showed class and impeccable taste.

He'd stumbled upon bowling as a way of alleviating his boredom after giving up boxing, and had very quickly become as much a star of the lanes as he'd been a champion in the ring.

'Accuracy, suppleness and touch are the three watchwords of bowling,' he said. 'And the same goes for marbles!' I felt a twinge of guilt at the mention of the marbles.

Once we had reached our destination, he parked his Peugeot 404 across three spaces, and we entered the bowling alley.

He was at the top of his game that night. He took a short run-up and then slid elegantly through his swing, opening up his body like a pair of scissors. The ball reluctantly left his hand, seemingly unwilling to take leave of his fingers, but then it slipped away with such grace, such gentleness that it looked as if it were gliding on a little cushion of air above the wooden floor. The scores lit up on a small screen, next to a dancing girl in a blue swimsuit. He racked up a series of a dozen strikes, and a small cluster of people slowly formed around our lane to watch.

Napoleon was concentrating on achieving a historic grand slam when a voice cut through the nervous silence: 'Don't mess it up, pal.'

My grandfather froze. Tossing the ball in the air, he fixed the onlookers with a steely glare. A group of jeering boys had obviously decided that they wanted to end the evening in hospital. Napoleon sucked it up, took a deep breath to calm himself and then returned to the top of his run-up.

'You'll be skittled soon, too, granddad!' another boy shouted.

The silence seemed to harden around us. Grandpa put down his ball and cleared his throat. He had an imperious, almost otherworldly air about him.

'Come on, pal,' he said in a loud voice. 'We're leaving. It stinks in here.'

'And?' Alexandre asked me the next day. 'How did it finish? Oh, come on, tell me what happened.'

'Are you really that interested?' I asked.

'Oh yeah! Go on, tell me.'

'Well ... We went out into the car park in the dark and the gang of boys followed us. They were cracking their knuckles.'

'Wow!' cried Alexandre. 'So you went back inside?'

'No way. My grandpa just said, "I usually only deal out beatings by appointment, but I'll make an exception this time. Who's first?"'

'And where were you?'

'I was sitting on the bonnet of the 404, taking care of my grandpa's bowling ball. It was like being at the cinema, you see. The only thing missing was the popcorn!'

'Weren't you scared? For your grandfather, I mean?'

I burst out laughing. 'Scared? What of? He told me, very calmly, "Sorry to keep you waiting, but this'll only take a few seconds." And bang! bang! One after the other, he laid them out cold. Just like that, without a second thought. You should have seen the thrashing they took! The kids were writhing and groaning on the ground, so my grandpa said, "Now get lost, if you want to make it out of here while you can still walk!"'

'What happened next?'

'They ran.'

'That's cool!' said Alexandre. 'You're a really good storyteller.'

Alexandre Rawcziik said very little about his family or his reasons for moving house and missing the start of the school year. It was clear to me that he hated the idea of someone finding out about his past. In spite of (or perhaps because of) his reluctance, most of the kids insisted on bombarding him with questions like 'Where are you from? What do your parents do? Are both your parents still alive?'

I admired the skills he had developed to evade such questions. He was almost as good at this game as he was at marbles. As a result, the other kids soon grew tired of pestering him. They accepted that they'd never find out anything about him and took their revenge by completely ignoring him: he simply didn't exist.

One peculiar quirk contributed to his exclusion. The others found this habit revolting, but I was intrigued by it. He observed and tracked insects, devoting entire breaktimes to keeping them out of harm's way and off the paths used by the other pupils. He knew their scientific names, and words like *coleoptera, chafer, manticora* and *lucanus cervus* soon seemed every bit as luminous, precious and poetic to me as Napoleon's colourful language.

We spent a lot of time together, even if was only on the

walk to school each day. He grew to trust me because I never enquired about his family. I didn't even mention Napoleon's marbles. I had felt awful about losing them, but it had never come up with Napoleon, and my grandfather had taught me to be a good sportsman. They were no longer mine, and I concluded I'd better forget about them.

However, that day, after my account of Napoleon's feats at the bowling alley, I saw Alexandre fish a bag out of his pocket. He opened it and stuck his hand inside.

'I like it when you tell me about your grandpa's adventures. You're a better storyteller than you are a marbles player. Choose one.'

'But—'

'Go on, take one. You can tell me more stories.'

7

I didn't see much of my father because he would leave home very early to go to work at the bank. As I lay in bed I'd hear his car start up. He'd rev the engine a bit, tune the radio and then drive off, tyres crunching on the gravel. I found this regularity reassuring. My mother would already be drawing by the time I got up. Sometimes I had the impression that she'd spent the whole night in the small studio she'd set up in a corner of the attic; it resembled a ship's cabin. I was the only one who could stand up straight in it, right in the middle, and I loved to nose about there and breathe in the scent of glue, varnish, pastels and paint.

She'd tried to hold down more conventional jobs, with strict working hours and bosses to answer to, but she'd always been fired after a few weeks at the most. Sometimes it was because she didn't keep to the agreed hours of employment or because she doodled all over files and documents or fell asleep at her desk. Generally, though, it was because no sooner was she hired than she lost the capacity to speak. She couldn't help it: not a sound would issue from her lips. She simply wasn't cut out for the world of work.

However, if she drew a flower, you'd feel as if you could smell its fragrance, and if you suffered from hay fever it made you want to sneeze. Her drawings were always bathed in sunlight whose warmth you could feel on your skin. She could also draw rain in an incredibly realistic manner. One of her sketchbooks was dedicated entirely to rain – drizzle, showers, downpours – and you could almost hear the raindrops on the roof, feel them on your skin and even smell the particular aroma of grass and trees wet with summer rain.

That morning, as so often, I climbed the stairs, trying not to make a sound so I could have the pleasure of surprising her, but without even turning round she cried, 'I can hear you. Failed again!'

She worked in the midst of organised chaos. Sheets and sheets of drawings formed precarious towers; stacks of all kinds of CDs and books balanced as if by magic; and the photos on the walls overlapped. In whichever direction you walked, you would trip over brightly coloured sketchbooks, and I wondered how such chaos could possibly give rise to drawings of such amazing clarity.

'Are you going to Napoleon's today?' she asked.

'Yep. We're going to start on the walls.'

'Ah yes, that's right,' she said with a wry smile. 'Your dad wasn't very pleased. Napoleon does overdo it sometimes.'

A few days ago Napoleon and I had visited a DIY store where we chose paint and other equipment which we charged to my father's account. Since they had the same name, his little scam had gone undetected.

'How is he?' she asked.

'Grandpa? Very well indeed. I have trouble keeping up with him!'

My mother was like the characters she drew – carefree and joyful, but also with a quiet melancholy they could never quite shake off. Her characters could veer from laughter to tears at the turn of a page. Once she wrote a book about a little girl who had been paralysed by some disease, but her illness had led her to discover drawing and painting. I was sure my mum was in fact telling her own story. What's more, she shared the little girl's name: Elea.

My mother dipped her brush in a jar of water and said to me in a tone of affected nonchalance, 'I know that you don't really want us to know what the two of you get up to together, but let us know if you ever need any help. There might come a time . . .'

She trailed off. There was a lingering silence. I realised she wasn't going to finish her sentence, and instead she picked up her brush again.

'What's your story about?' I asked.

She flashed me a mischievous smile. 'I don't like people to know what I'm up to, either. You can read it when the time comes.'

'Soon?'

'I don't know.'

I put my foot on the top of the stairs, but suddenly I stopped. 'Mum, there is one thing I can't get my head around.'

'What's that?' she called out, not looking round.

'I don't really understand why Napoleon left Grandma. She'd surely have agreed to a fresh start, and he seems to think about her non-stop. He doesn't say so, but I can tell.'

Her brush slipped on the paper and slithered to a halt. She waited a few seconds before answering. 'Go and help Napoleon, my love. An emperor always has his reasons.'

It was only a short walk to the part of town where Napoleon lived. His house was much smaller than my parents', and its blue shutters reminded me of those fishermen's huts you find by the sea.

The living room was thick with steam when I entered. We had gathered the furniture in the centre of the room a few days earlier. Napoleon was holding at arm's length a wallpaper steamer that was roaring like a dragon; he looked like Hercules slaying the Hydra. Long strips of wallpaper were hanging from the walls, and Endov was snapping at them.

'Everything OK, pal?'

'Great. How about you?'

'Fan-tastic. Absolutely full of beans. I'm shedding my skin too. Go and open the window. I can't see a thing in here.'

The steam spilled outside, the white clouds evaporating almost instantaneously into the air. It was a scene my mother might have drawn.

Napoleon unplugged the steamer and tossed me a scraper. I caught it.

'Nice catch! Next we apply some filler and then we'll get started on the painting this afternoon. Never waste a minute, right, pal?'

'Got it.'

'Throw yourself into things head first. Always catch them by surprise! Surprise is the key to winning a battle. Otherwise, the enemy gets organised and things get difficult.'

Perching on his stepladder, he made full use of his graceful, long limbs. I was overwhelmed by the smell of paste and damp wallpaper.

'Emperor, oh my emperor,' I said. 'Did you know Rocky well?'

His scraper stopped moving and for a few seconds he kept his eyes shut.

'Rocky? A bit ... We would occasionally run into each other in the changing rooms. We trained at the same gym. He was an amazing guy! He used a sack filled with mail as a punch bag. He couldn't read, so he didn't bother to open his post. That's why he always said that the more fan mail he received, the stronger he felt. He was the only boxer ever to hang up his gloves entirely undefeated. IN-VIN-CIBLE, Rocky was.'

'You could have beaten him.'

'Let's change the subject, pal.'

'Did Rocky have any children? Did he?'

Napoleon cleaned his scraper. He was as thin as the strips of paper strewn across the floor. I suddenly realised that Josephine's scent was gone, as if it had been carried off by the clouds of steam. I felt lonely with Napoleon and I was immediately ashamed to feel that way.

'Children?' he muttered. 'Don't know. Come on, time for some education.' He tossed his scraper into the bowl with all the elegance of a basketball player who knows that his throw will find the hoop.

The small transistor radio crackled for a few seconds before the presenter's voice grew clear.

We liked absolutely everything about this game show. The voice of the presenter, who geed up his audience with unflagging enthusiasm to shout the immortal words: 'Welcome to *WHO WANTS TO WIN A THOUSAND EURO-O-OS?!*' We loved the unbearable silence after each question, the three notes signalling that time for deliberation was over, and above all the hesitation as a contestant considered whether to stop or carry on playing, with the crowd screaming in the background, 'JACK-POT! JACK-POT! JACK-POT!'

'I'll stop there,' a contestant would sometimes say.

'Oh, come on, you wimp!' Napoleon would shout.

Napoleon had got into the habit of listening to this game show while driving his taxi. He would stop by the verge or on the hard shoulder of the motorway without any regard for his passengers or the rush they might be in when the final round of the game took place.

This long-running show had had a series of different presenters, and my grandfather got them mixed up. Incapable of remembering which of them had retired, who was dead and which one was currently asking the questions, he would lump them all together as 'What's-his-face'.

That particular day Napoleon opened a tin of sardines. He picked one up by its tail with his thumb and forefinger and dangled it in front of Endov, who wolfed it down with a single snap of his jaws. With a fin still protruding from his mouth, the dog rested his head on Grandpa's thigh. My grandfather slapped the remaining sardines onto two slices of bread and handed me one.

'I should've been a chef,' he said, biting into his snack.

It was time for the first question.

'Now this is a tough question, so watch out. Why is there no Nobel Prize in Mathematics?' the presenter said.

The seconds ticked away.

'Think hard about this one,' the presenter murmured. 'It's a tough question, and the answer's a little surprising . . . '

Napoleon thought about it, rocking his head from side to side. 'Do you know?' he asked me.

I shrugged and shook my head.

The three notes rang out, clear and cruel.

'Well, listen to this. The wife of the inventor of the famous prize had a mathematician lover, and Nobel refused to crown the mathematical genius to spite her,' the presenter announced.

This was the kind of anecdote that delighted my grandfather.

'Hear that, Endov? What a bunch of jokers these egg-heads are!'

He listened closely, his curiosity suddenly piqued, then frowned and moved closer to the radio.

'Shh,' he said.

'I didn't say anything. You were the one who—'

'I said shush. Crikey, did you hear that?'

I had heard. In a few days' time the programme was going to be recorded near us. I was as overjoyed about this as Napoleon was. The presenter continued to praise our town.

'Ah, the forest, the castle and . . . um . . . the gym,' the presenter said.

'It had to happen sometime,' my grandfather declared. 'It took him long enough to decide to come and pay us a visit.'

He switched off the radio, propped his elbows on

his knees and rested his chin on his palms. He seemed very far away.

Suddenly he beckoned for me to come closer and said quietly, 'I wonder about something, you know.'

'Oh yeah, and what's that?'

'I wonder if this What's-his-face presenter is truly happy. Always trekking from one town to the next without ever being able to sit down and rest his backside for five minutes, all to ask people questions. Is that any sort of life?'

'Maybe he likes asking questions?'

'Well, I'd get fed up with it,' he said, 'and I'm sure he's sick of it too.' Napoleon paused as if a sadness was washing over him, then he quickly pulled himself together. 'All right – a little arm-wrestle to limber up before we head off again!'

Our two hands clasped. Straining muscles. Fake grimaces. My arm tracing a semicircle. Nothing I could do. He was unbeatable.

'Easy-peasy!' said Napoleon. 'You won't be beating me anytime soon.'

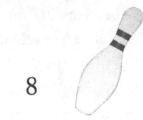

8

A few days later I walked in on Napoleon washing Endov in the bathroom. The dog was hidden in a cloud of foam, but stoically putting up with the indignity.

'You're washing the dog, Grandpa?'

'Wow, you're observant! Very impressive!'

'You're cleaning him with washing-up liquid?'

'It does a very good job. Did you catch a whiff of the fragrance? Mediterranean Pine! I've just finished.'

Endov leaped out of the bathtub and disappeared, leaving a trail of foam in his wake.

'Aren't we going to carry on with the decorating?' I asked.

Napoleon wiped his hands meticulously before answering. 'We're going to take a break. We've got to be ready.'

'All right,' I said. I thought for a couple of seconds before enquiring, 'Ready for what?'

'Ready to strike. A major strike. An historic strike.' And he banged his fist three times on the side of the bathtub to emphasise his words.

'It can't possibly go wrong! I've calculated everything right down to the tiniest detail, pal. We have the whole weekend ahead of us. You and Endov will be my backups.'

'There's one thing I want to know, Grandpa.'

'Go ahead and ask. We need to make sure everything's clear before we start.'

'Why do you want to kidnap What's-his-face?'

That was his major strike: kidnapping the presenter, just before he arrived at the gym.

'Why? Think about it for a second, pal. Because he needs to be freed. I know, I know – don't give me that look. Freed from inside his little radio set and from all the questions he asks. We have to break him out of his jail so he can live a little!'

I was stunned. He had such an irresistible way of expressing things and an infectious energy, no matter how crazy this suggestion was.

'He won't agree to it, you know,' I said.

'Of course he won't agree. It wouldn't be a kidnapping if he did. But he'll thank us later.'

'If you say so . . .' I was quietly stunned by this plan. I was used to going along with Napoleon's madcap ideas, and I think at this stage I didn't fully believe he would execute a plan like this, but the route was there, the getaway, the gear and the method: it was all laid out, every single detail. To top it all off, the whole plan hinged on Endov.

My grandfather paced up and down his living room between the bowls and pots of paint, as if he were on stage. He moved his hands excitedly and his eyes seemed wild.

'We stop his car, he gets out and then, *thwack* – he vanishes. In a matter of seconds.'

'Where will we put him?'

'In the boot of the 404. A big boot like that has to serve some purpose at least once. But there's no way we can wing something like this; we'll have to practise hard. So, pal, we start tomorrow.'

He made a sign with his hand as if he were zipping up his lips.

'But hold your tongue. Don't go and spoil everything.'

I held my tongue, all right. Kept it on a short leash. All tied up, like one of the chickens my mother bought at the butcher's for the Sunday roast, as if to stop it from running away. Officially I went to my grandfather's to carry on with the decorating, and each evening, when my parents enquired about our progress, I would reply evasively about levelling substances and fillers, smoothing with sandpaper, painting ornamentations and marouflage. I showed them my hands, which Napoleon daubed with paint before I went home. I was a little ashamed of my lies, but Napoleon seemed so wedded to this 'major strike' that I did not contemplate betraying him, and perhaps a part of me still didn't think it would actually happen. I thought that perhaps it was all a game – like the wrestling and the play-fighting.

In actual fact, Napoleon drove me along an old canal towpath on the outskirts of town where various more or less abandoned barges were rotting away. In his opinion, it was a dead cert that the presenter's car would arrive via the main road that intersected with the track where the 404 was hidden.

'He'll come from the south,' Napoleon declared, 'and head north towards the gym hall. He won't go to the trouble of taking a different route.'

I enjoyed seeing my grandfather in this mood. No time to waste on discussing things. Three days of rehearsals.

'I've got everything planned. Down to the last detail.'

He dug his hand into a big bag of dog biscuits, clapped, stamped his foot and scattered the biscuits on the edge of the road in the precise spot where Endov was to learn to play dead.

'A squirt of ketchup to make it look right,' Napoleon explained. 'What's-his-face will get out of his car.'

'Are you sure?'

'Positive. He once said that he had a dog and that he loved dogs.'

This did sound like a strong argument. Napoleon could see that I was wavering.

'However, if you have any doubts about my leadership or my strategy . . .'

'I was only asking!'

He looked pensively at the sky and tapped his chin with his index finger. 'I recall that he talked about his dog on 17 January 1979 at Valenciennes.'

'You have one heck of a memory, Grandpa!'

For three days I had played the role of What's-his-face getting out of his car to help Endov, who was now trained to lie down on command. Tongue lolling, he played the perfect corpse.

Napoleon came up behind me and dragged me away, with his hand over my mouth to gag me. In less than no time, I found myself in the boot.

Pressing the button on his stopwatch, Napoleon announced, 'He's locked in the boot within seventeen seconds. Brilliant.' He gave the side of his car a slap. 'Nice set of wheels, this 404.'

I found these days helping my grandfather to prepare his major strike troubling. It was clear the plan was going to happen, but it was as if he were treading a tightrope over a void – yet we laughed and had a good time. Organising What's-his-face's kidnapping was becoming a great source of fun and play for us, and my grandfather was in better spirits.

At noon Napoleon opened a tin of sardines. He tossed one to Endov, who caught it in mid-air, and then lined the others up on the blade of his penknife in order to lay them out on slices of bread. The soft centre absorbed the oil, which eventually dripped onto our thighs.

'Grandpa,' I said. 'We put What's-his-face in the boot, right?'

'You've got it.'

'OK, but then what? What do we do next?'

He smiled with the knowing air of a man with a water-tight plan. 'Ha ha, I told you I'm leaving nothing to chance, pal. I've got it all worked out.'

Napoleon pointed to one of the barges moored on the canal bank. 'See that barge over there? We stick him on it.'

'But he'll escape.'

'I'd be surprised ... because I'll be steering it down the canal.' He laughed so hard that he dropped a sardine.

'So you mean you—'

'Exactly. I'm getting out of here. Not for very long. A few weeks, just enough to get some fresh air. It'll really wind up Wet Blanket, too! He can try his damnedest to keep me under control. Why are you looking at me like that?'

'Do you know how to sail a barge?'

He shrugged. 'It'll be a cinch. Can't be much harder than driving a car.'

'And where are you going to take What's-his-face on your barge?'

'To Venice. It'll make a change from his little transistor. At long last he'll see something other than rows of seats in gyms or community hall toilets where there's never any bog roll. The wide world! The joys of life, culture and art! I just hope he doesn't ask too many questions.'

A smile played on my lips. My imagination started to run wild and I saw Napoleon's barge floating along the Grand Canal and heard the presenter badgering him with questions. He was right – it was going to be a major strike, a thousand-euro bid that would remain ingrained on people's memories. I loved it when he believed he could take on the world. I convinced myself the presenter might even end up enjoying it.

Napoleon glanced at his watch. 'Speaking of What's-his-face . . .' He searched for the correct frequency on the car radio. The presenter's voice was fuzzy and indistinct at first, but then it became sharper. One question followed the other. Maybe he really was waiting for us – waiting to be rescued.

'Be patient, me old mucker,' Napoleon said. 'Your thousand-euro reward will be along in next to no time.

'What do you mean, Grandpa?'

'We'll hold him ransom for a thousand euros.'

'Really?'

'Yes, we're on our way!'

His voice seemed slow and sad. 'We're on our way!'

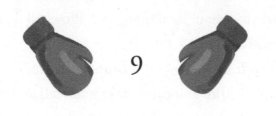

9

And then we were indeed on our way. That Wednesday
Napoleon looked alert and alive as he glanced back at
his house one last time. I had had trouble sleeping. I felt
a mixture of impatience and simmering anxiety; I wondered if I'd done the right thing by holding my tongue.
But Napoleon's unshakeable confidence swept away
my doubts.

'The final straight, pal!'

We set off for the towpath in the 404, which was loaded
with stocks of dog biscuits and a cargo of ketchup. Endov
was posing on the back seat like a Hollywood film star.
Napoleon pulled on the handbrake and tapped the 404's
little clock to make sure it was working properly.

'Everything's running to plan,' he cried with delight.
'Half an hour ahead of schedule.'

The two of us shuffled around the car. He checked the tyres by giving them a kick. I followed his lead.

He stopped beside the boot with his hand on his chin. 'I'm wondering about something, pal. How tall do you think What's-his-face is?'

'No idea. It isn't easy to tell from the radio.'

'Imagine the fun and games if he's too tall and we have to leave his feet sticking out? We've got to check.' In a flash he'd opened the boot. 'I'm going to step inside, pal, so we can check. Come on, we need to hurry.' He already had one leg over the rim. Lying diagonally, he just about fitted. 'Close the lid, pal, just so I can see what it's like in here.'

Snap. Silence. Not a sound. A few seconds passed.

'Grandpa? Are you still in there?'

'Where else would I be? Open up.'

I smiled as Endov gazed at me, then said, 'I can't. You've got the keys.'

After a few seconds of silence my grandfather cursed, 'Oh, bloody flipping hell!' He raged, struggled, stamped his feet and slammed his fists into the boot lid, but it made no difference: he was stuck.

'We're going to miss him,' he yelled. 'We're going to miss him! We were within touching distance of a work of genius.'

The car rocked back and forth, its shock absorbers squealing. Minutes passed. Quarter of an hour. Half an hour.

'It was all worked out to the last second,' he lamented. 'And now it's ruined. Sod those thousand euros!'

'We're going to have to fetch help,' I said. 'Dad must have a second set of keys.'

'Never, do you hear me? Ne-ver!'

'You're going to need to eat.'

'I've got enough dog biscuits to last me a century.'

But we could not carry on as we were. First, cyclists and pedestrians began to think that there was something fishy about a ten-year-old boy talking to the boot of a Peugeot 404, and then Napoleon began to cough and rail and choke. Also, I was hungry, thirsty and scared.

'I need a piss,' Napoleon finally announced.

After almost an hour we struck gold. Two police officers drew up in their patrol car, and the uniformed figures came wandering down the track. Endov immediately slumped onto his side and played dead.

I alerted my grandfather, who started to giggle like a madman.

'Why are you laughing?'

'Because.'

'Because what?'

Between hiccups he managed to say, 'If they can't get me out, they can't lock me up!'

The two police officers decided that my grandfather and I were up to something weird, and I was obliged to give them my father's phone number. It was either that or a trip to the police station.

My father arrived a few minutes later brandishing a spare set of keys and conferred with the officers until they gradually softened their tone.

One of them eventually admitted, 'My dad's getting on a bit too.'

My father turned the key in the lock of the boot, but still it refused to open. It was clear that Napoleon was blocking it from the inside.

'Come out now,' my father ordered.

'No chance,' Napoleon shouted. 'Haven't you got work to do?'

'Yes, lots, but I'm not leaving until you come out.'

'You can go, do you hear?'

'I don't believe this!' my father exclaimed. 'I drop everything to come and rescue you, and all you can do is tell me to clear off?'

My grandfather burst out laughing from inside the boot. 'Rescue me? Are you having a laugh?'

'Of course I'm rescuing you. How else will you get out of there?'

'I was doing just fine without you. We were just playing, that's all.'

'What exactly were you playing, the two of you?'

'Hide and seek!'

'Hide and seek? In the boot of a car by the side of the canal?'

Tired from all the excitement, Endov was playing dead again.

'So is your dog playing too?' my father asked. He brought his fist down on the lid of the boot, making a small dent. 'How old are you, Dad?' he cried.

'Old enough to show you who's boss!' was Napoleon's reply.

10

The next day Napoleon peeled a picture of the Grand Canal off his fridge. He'd stuck it there a week ago while we rehearsed our plan.

'We're not going to let them get us down, pal. Who cares about Venice anyway? I'm told it stinks there.'

He stared at the photo for a long time and then in a single movement crumpled it into a ball and chucked it into the bin. Next he set about prising open a gigantic pot of paint.

'After all,' he said, 'What's-his-face's nothing but a voice.'

Although we'd been forced to abort it, our adventure had some positive outcomes. Napoleon had rediscovered his house as if he'd just returned home from a long holiday. The decorating awaited us, the brushes stretched out asking to be used and the rollers were desperate to be rolled.

Once the paint pot was open, Napoleon used a stick to mix the contents.

'It all goes to show one thing, pal,' he said. 'Always be cautious and never let down your guard. One momentary lapse of attention and you're finished. Never let anyone box you in!'

He ran one of the clean brushes over my face.

'You're tickling my eyes!'

Through my half-open eyelids I could see Napoleon chuckling and I felt that this moment would stick in my memory for ever.

'And don't skimp,' he said. 'Be generous. Give it a good lick of paint – the bank's paying! We're going to apply several coats and do it with great care. We've got lots of time. No hurry. That way we won't have to touch it again for at least five years.'

'Ten years, even.'

'Yeah, ten years.'

The only consequence of our recent adventure was a faint scratch on Napoleon's forehead, and a twinge of regret that he never mentioned, but that I could sense was growing inside him, worsening each time the game show came on the radio. Eventually he switched the radio off for several days. In late mornings Napoleon would stretch out his hand – from force of habit – to turn on the radio, only to pull his fingers back as if he feared getting burnt.

'Damn it!'

Even later on, when he'd resumed listening to his favourite programme, he did so with a distant look in his eyes, as if he was imagining sailing along the Grand Canal.

Napoleon was never silent for very long when he painted. He always derived great pleasure from telling me the story of how he'd become a cabbie. I was hearing it for the thousandth time. It had required the intervention of fate.

'One day I was driving back from a fight at Wagram Hall. It was very late, at least two in the morning. I stopped at a red light. I didn't want to go home, you know what I mean ... And just then, bang, a lady knocks on the window and asks me if I am free. Very young and very pretty she is. I say yes. What? I was as free as a bird. So she opens the back door. That lady was Josephine.'

Napoleon interpreted this as the call of destiny. He decided his second life would be that of a married taxi driver.

'When you want to start a new life, there's no need to rack your brains for ages. I put my gloves in the glove compartment – and *avanti*! You can't imagine how many different people I gave rides to, pal. Rich folk, poor folk. Chatty, taciturn, young, old, sad or joyful. And dickheads – all manner of dickheads.'

What he liked most was being confided in by his passengers, saying things they couldn't say to anyone else, and feeling as if he knew them better than anybody else.

'I gave rides to men who'd just become fathers or who

were going into hospital, and others who were leaving for the ends of the earth to escape the law. Some were laughing, while others cried.'

At the beginning, certain passengers recognised him; they'd seen him fight somewhere or spotted his photo in the paper. He signed autographs. People asked him about his mysterious defeat to Rocky.

He missed the boxing scene a bit, but he regarded Rocky's death as a sign that he should hang up his gloves, too. That day, as paint fumes filled the room, he added, 'You'll understand one day, pal. I owe my greatest moments of joy in life to Rocky.'

What did he mean? His voice had taken on that particular tone that ruled out any follow-up questions.

'This is all getting far too serious,' he said. 'Put on some music, pal. To cheer us up. It's important to work in a good atmosphere and in a happy mood – especially when you're starting a new life.'

I turned on the radio, and the voice of Claude François rang out over those pots of paint.

Napoleon started to sing along with the words and to swipe his brush in time to the beat. Every fifteen seconds he'd dip it into the enormous pot with a little wiggle of his hips. He was building up to something – and all of a sudden he exploded! He rotated so that he had both feet firmly planted on the floor, wide apart, and then tossed away the brush, which flew in lazy spirals across the room. Throwing his head back, he executed a variety of whirling motions with his hands, raised his arms to the heavens and waggled his elbows as if he were attempting to take off. He lifted one thigh in the air, wriggled the other, hopped on the spot and twisted his backside before thrusting it out behind him.

'Watch this, pal. Not bad, eh?' He was rolling his shoulders, lifting his chin, stepping forwards and backwards and then capped it all off with a stationary spin.

Claude François continued singing about being hungrier than a barracuda. 'Barracuda . . .' Napoleon sang, returning to the chorus with his mouth wide open.

I was struck dumb with admiration. Incredibly muscular and as wiry as a giant insect, he was twisting, stamping his heel on the floor and linking his hands behind his back before waving them in the air.

'You're a great dancer! Where did you learn?'

'On Broadway!'

He paused for a moment to pull his jeans above his navel, adding, 'You ain't seen nothin' yet. Just wait for the chorus!'

It came – the chorus about the slide on the pyramids – and Napoleon put his arms above his head and waved them from side to side, as if in farewell, to the immortal melody of the sirens of Alexandria.

'Wo-wo-wo-wo!' he echoed.

'You're a natural, Grandpa,' I cried, tears of laughter in my eyes. 'You're the barracuda! You're the champion, you're the emperor and no one will ever steal your crown.'

At that precise moment, as I was later to relate the scene to Alexandre, I genuinely felt that I was in the presence of an immortal. Someone who would always be with me; someone who would beat me in an arm-wrestle for as long as I lived. Napoleon was one of those people whose absence it was impossible to imagine.

All of a sudden I froze.

'Wait!' I roared.

Too late. Completely absorbed in his series of increasingly daring dance moves, Napoleon had stepped on a strip of wallpaper streaked with wet glue and paint. He skidded on it as if at an ice rink and crashed into the furniture gathered in the centre of the room.

Not in the least put out by this commotion, Claude François continued to holler.

But Grandpa was gesticulating wildly, lying on his back like a beetle that couldn't right itself. Part of me wanted to laugh, but this felt serious.

'Are you all right, Grandpa?'

'Don't call me that.'

I imitated a referee giving the count in the ring, 'One ... two ...'

'Stop it, boy. I'm counting.'

'Counting what?'

'My bones. I feel like I've lost half of them. Do I look OK from the outside?'

'Yes, I think so.'

'Can't you shut the great Claude François up for a minute? His barracudas are getting on my nerves.'

Silence returned. Grandpa looked in a pretty bad way. He was gritting his teeth and groaning.

'Come on, pal. Help me to my feet. Don't let your emperor down. He's going through a bad patch. The opponent took us by surprise. See? A momentary lack of attention and . . .'

'We'll get our revenge.'

'Right you are. Let's not give in to pessimism.'

I tried to pull him to his feet, but he was too heavy and I was afraid that he would shatter into small pieces. He looked tiny down there on the floor, barely larger than a child.

'Give the paint pot a tug. I want my foot back.'

In the heat of the moment I hadn't noticed that he had plunged his foot into the paint pot where it had got stuck. I grabbed it with both hands and tugged with all my might, but it was hopeless.

'OK, pal, what do we do in a situation like this?'

'Usually, my emperor, we would call on our allies.'

From the look in his eye and the frown on his face I realised that he was trying to picture in his mind all the people who might come to his aid. But his court was deserted; all his friends were gone.

Embarrassed, he finally declared, 'You're thinking of *him*? Wet Blanket?'

'I don't see any other options.'

'You don't seriously think I'm going to ask for his help?'

The house had grown darker. Daylight was fading and shadows were prowling about like ghosts. In the middle of our decorating, with the walls covered in paint and the floor strewn with scraps of paper and chunks of plaster, the house seemed abandoned. It looked as if Josephine had left centuries ago.

'What else can we do, emperor? Sometimes you have to swallow your pride.'

'I'd rather you brought me a glass of water. That'd be more useful and I'll be able to think straight.'

He took a good long swig, but things were no different afterwards.

'What a stupid song that is! Barracuda, my arse!' He was very pale now and his forehead was slick with sweat.

'Are you in pain?' I asked.

'Not at all. But I do think my backbone's in bits, pal. If you see the odd vertebra lying around, pick it up because it belongs to me!'

I pretended to scour the floor, but then I sat down on the stepladder.

'Why don't you want to ring him?'

'Are you going on about Wet Blanket again?'

'Yes, I think we need reinforcements.'

'No way. I'll be back on my feet in fifteen minutes, and we'll go bowling this evening.'

'I have an idea. We'll do heads or tails.'

'All right,' he said. 'Tails we don't call him, and heads . . .

we don't call him either!' He cackled at this, but his cackles soon faded to a mumble. 'So that he can deport me to one of those fully equipped houses . . . I know he's asking around. You know what he's like: he takes his time and does things methodically. One day, if I don't watch out, he'll harpoon me – wham! Before you can say Jack Robinson, I'll be put away in one of their old people's camps stinking of dirty underwear. I don't fancy ending up with old people. I'm going to stay here and get by on my own. All on my own with my faithful aide-de-camp until . . . until . . . '

'Until what?'

'Until people stop harassing me, that's what. Where are you going?'

'To the toilet. Don't move.'

'Shame, I was thinking of going out dancing.'

I closed the door to stare at the photo of Rocky on the wall. Fists thudding into flesh. Boots skipping over the canvas. I looked Rocky in the eye. I'd known this photo since I was a toddler. I got the feeling he was talking to me. I didn't believe the match had been rigged. I thought Napoleon had wavered. But Napoleon never wavered: Napoleon always fought to the bitter end; Napoleon never gave up. Napoleon was my emperor, and I would never give up on him either. If he was lying to me, then it must be for a good reason. I loved him as well as his lies. I loved Napoleon.

*

'Ah, you're back!' cried Napoleon. 'I thought you must have fallen down a hole.'

I crouched down beside him. 'We have to call for help.'

His glare lashed out like a rabid dog.

'I'm scared, Grandpa. Scared for you.'

He gave me such a tender smile then that I thought I was going to burst into tears, and he mumbled, 'You're right. A good soldier knows when to admit he's afraid. Call him, but try to preserve your dignity. We're going to make a temporary tactical retreat, that's all. I'm not calling for help. He's not going to catch me with my trousers down. I'm offering him an alliance.'

'Of course. A strategic alliance.'

'Yeah, that's pretty good. A strategic alliance. We pull the wool over our opponent's eyes. We trick him. We'll come back even stronger! Ever heard of Joe Louis?'

'No.'

'An American boxer. That was his big thing. He'd pretend he was flagging to fool his opponents.'

'Well, we'll do the same.'

'Yep. We're going to pull the wool over Wet Blanket's eyes!'

My father picked up the phone immediately. He didn't sound surprised to hear me.

'I'm on my way,' he said with a sigh, as if he'd been waiting for the call, fully dressed and with the car keys in his hand.

During the half an hour or so it would take him to drive

over, I tried to find out why Napoleon and my father had drifted so far apart over the years. I thought my grandpa would refuse to answer, but despite the circumstances, he was actually pretty forthcoming.

'I tried to prepare him for life,' he said. 'I tried to get him to take boxing seriously, but you should've seen him in the ring: it was ridiculous. He just stood there with his arms dangling by his sides, gazing around. Everyone was wetting themselves laughing. I was so embarrassed!'

'You wanted him to be like you?'

He hesitated for a second before replying. 'No,' he said. 'I didn't want him to be like me, but I didn't want him to be so different either. He was only interested in stuff like arithmetic, chemistry, literature. And stamps! They were everywhere! All the books he devoured, for God's sake! I didn't realise there were so many books out there. I had to leave him at the library while I went down to the bookies to make a bet. See what I mean? He wasn't quick-witted and he never got into fights, but as soon as there was any home- work to be done he would throw himself into it headlong like a madman. I took him to boxing matches but he'd fall asleep after the second round, and when he woke up he'd start blubbing because he was behind with his geometry. You'd have thought he'd drawn up a list of all the things to please me and make me proud, just so he could do the exact opposite. But actually it's my fault, pal.'

'Your fault?'

'Yeah, he went off the rails. I should have watched the company he was keeping, shown greater authority. Luckily, you should turn out better than he did. This kind of thing apparently skips a generation.' He groaned with pain, then arched an eyebrow. 'What mark did you get in arithmetic?'

'Arithmetic? Three out of twenty, Grandpa.'

He gave me a thumbs-up. 'And your last dictation?'

'Thirty-seven mistakes, excluding accents!'

'No way? Now you're bragging.'

'No, Grandpa, it's true!'

'You're consistent with your homework?'

'Oh yeah, Grandpa. Consistent as anything: I never do it.'

'How about detentions?'

'Half a dozen since the beginning of the year.'

'Not bad, but you can do better. Do you get your homework book signed?'

'Never, Grandpa.'

'What's your technique?'

'A copy of my mum's signature on a piece of tracing paper.'

My lies amused him, but did he believe them? Who cared!

'My emperor,' I said, 'tell me the o—'

'The old story . . . ?'

'Oh, go on.'

'But I've told it to you at least fifty times already. Well, all right then, but this is the last time.'

At some stage in the past – I had only a vague recollection of when – my father's job entailed making presentations to various professional organisations. They would include figures, percentages, graphs, details of investments and so forth.

'That sort of stuff, pal. Not exactly a barrel of laughs – more like a vale of tears.'

Grandpa had given him a nice dark tie for his birthday, and my father had seen this gift as an olive branch.

'Thanks, Dad,' he'd said with a tremor in his voice. 'I'll wear it for my speech tomorrow.'

'And I'll come along to listen.'

'Really, Dad?'

He was probably happy that Napoleon was finally taking his career seriously. In fact, though, it didn't work out as he had hoped. Dad had been greeted with sarcastic heckling from the crowd of bankers and VIPs who were attending his speech. A murmur ran through the audience, who became restless and started laughing. It turned out that his tie had become fluorescent under the lights – he became known as the banker with the novelty tie and no one paid any attention to his speech. Dad had come home like a raging bull, ready to smash anything within reach.

'You humiliated me this time. We're finished.'

'Humiliated? There's no need to overreact,' Napoleon had said. 'You made people laugh for once.'

This story provoked a sadness in me, and yet I couldn't stop asking my grandfather to tell it. I imagined how delighted my father must have been by the thought that Napoleon was finally showing an interest in his world – and then his embarrassment and his disappointment in front of the audience. My heart broke for him.

'Why did you play that trick on him?'

'I had my reasons,' he snapped. 'I gave up after that. I realised it was no use and that I'd made a mess of everything.'

'What do you mean "everything"?'

I thought he was going to start sobbing. Then we heard the sound of a car engine and a door slamming.

'Here he is,' muttered Napoleon. 'He can't get here fast enough when there's a chance of seeing me down for the count.'

'So what happened next?' Alexandre asked me, his eyes shining with excitement.

'We took him to the hospital. He didn't want to stay there – you should have heard him screaming in the corridor! He kept on yelling that all he needed was a couple of aspirin.'

'Is it serious?'

'A broken spine, although he won't accept that diagnosis. He accuses my dad of scheming and paying the doctors to put him away.'

'And all that stuff about your homework and marks and detentions was untrue, right?'

'It isn't true. In fact it's exactly the opposite: I always do my homework. I enjoy it. It's just that, you know, when I'm with Napoleon, it's as if I'm a different person. As if I were like him. We get to go on adventures. He likes me because I reckon he knows I'm like him. It gives him hope.'

'What about Endov?'

'Endov's at my house. We weren't going to leave him all alone. My mum's drawing him. She says he's a very patient model.'

He stopped and reached into his jacket pocket. He always wore the same clothes – the velvet jacket, the trousers with holes at the knees, the old trainers with worn-out soles – so I guessed that his family probably didn't have much money.

'You told that story well,' he said. 'Take another marble.'

Then he cast his eyes down at the ground. A small insect was moving about next to his shoe and he picked it up.

'Poor thing,' said Alexandre. 'He's fighting, but he's all alone. He could be crushed at any moment.'

A letter from Grandma

My darling boy,

My darling, I've been gone some time now and I've decided to give you my news in writing because the phone isn't handy for doing it, you forget lots of things and when you hang up you think I should have said that, that and that, and also writing helps pass the time, it's true you have to choose your words, look for a stamp and an envelope and run to the post box, it's almost a sport in its own right, but you will see that I have some trouble with punctuation, my full stops aren't up to the task, but you'll understand all the same, same thing with the mistakes, try to ignore them

I've had time, so much time, that I don't know what to do with it any more, if I could sell all the time I have on my hands I'd be a millionaire, those first days I didn't realise I'd have so much time to spend, just the opposite in fact, I didn't have a minute to myself, I was running around, arranging the house,

tidying away all my belongings, planting some things
in the garden and pulling out others, I didn't have
any time to think of your brute of a grandfather or
you or anyone else, even me

After a week there was nothing left to do and
I started to get the blues, navy blues, I had them
when I got up and I went to bed feeling blue too,
and in between I couldn't stop crying because of the
memories, they're the real enemy when you're on your
own, I was crying so much I thought it was raining, so
I had to give myself a good talking-to.

You see your grandfather isn't someone you can
forget just like that, with a click of your fingers,
when you've lived all your life with a hurricane it
feels strange when it suddenly stops, you have to
examine the damage and start fixing it, there are
cracks all over,

Even if he's a bit of a tiresome old egomaniac, he's
still someone you can't help loving for your whole life,
and don't go thinking I don't know what's going on
inside his nutty head, and one day you'll know too

So I poked my nose outside and tried to catch
up with some old friends, though most of them
had gone off God knows where, I found 3 in the
cemetery which isn't very helpful when you feel like
a chat, so at the end of the day I only have 2 left
nearby, the 2 toughest biddies, the ones I couldn't
stand at school, I've started going round to their
houses for tea, one of them farts all the time, every
couple of minutes I swear, I couldn't stop laughing

and between guffs she speaks ill of every man and
woman, old or young, and even animals, while
the other makes a sort of neighing noise every 10
seconds and says 'I could kill a roast', all that one
can think of is eating, roasted in the others' farts,
and I was fed up so I stopped going.

Speaking of animals I've taken to having a little
flutter to pass the time, I fill out my betting slip
every morning over a cup of coffee, I never thought
I'd do this, I don't have a clue about horses so I fill it
in at random but so far I've won nothing; yesterday
I wanted to buy a special magazine to get some
information, a sort of Betting for Dummies, and I
chose one from the rack at the newsagent's, when I
went to study it at home it wasn't about betting at
all, nothing like, someone must have put it back in
the wrong place, because it's full of classified ads,
lonely hearts looking for a companion, not a dog,
but a man, at first I wanted to take it back, as I'm
looking for a horse, not a man, but unfortunately I
read the first ad and then the second, and I was still
reading at midnight. Old men, young men, small,
tall, rich, poor, there are all kinds who in order to
get picked say: I'm like this, I'm like that, I like
this and I hate that, you'd never think but once
you stick your nose in it you can't pull it out again,
you're mesmerised. It comes out every Tuesday. And
tomorrow is Tuesday.

Big kisses,
Your loving grandma

PS. If that brute Napoleon asks if you've heard
from me, be a dear and say no, I know he'll call
me one day

PPS. I think PSs are classy

PPPS. If you meet the person who invented full stops,
stick your tongue out at him for me

11

Napoleon's room was on the top floor of the hospital. He had a panoramic view from his window, which was sealed shut. Railway tracks followed the banks of the Seine, which wound through tree-covered hills. Further away, on the hazy horizon, you could make out the runways of an airport on which a constant procession of glinting planes converged.

My father had paid a little extra for Napoleon to have his own room, and he had immediately plugged in the television. As soon as he arrived, my father suggested calling Josephine.

'If you let her know, you'd better get ready to run. Really, you're no good at most things, but you're a champion when it comes to humiliating me! One sniff of weakness and you start to get ideas. You're like a hyena.'

I paid him a visit the day after his admission. Without so much as greeting me he said, 'Your father is the first on the scene whenever there's a chance of gagging me. I'm sure he'd have shopped me to the Gestapo during the war.'

'Did you fight in the war?'

'No chance. I was in America when it broke out, so I stayed there. I'm not mad. I had no time for their little arguments. I like a fight, but only between gentlemen.'

'Did you meet Rocky over there?'

'Yep. At the start of the war. We trained at the same gym.'

He was so skinny that he barely made a bump in the sheet, but he looked very handsome with his head of thick white hair. He turned his head sideways to stare at the window.

'You see, pal, when you've lived a little like me – I didn't say when you're old; I mean when you've reached a certain level of maturity – lots of things strike you as very odd.'

His arm reached out towards the window, as if it were rising of its own accord, lifted by a pulley mechanism concealed in the ceiling.

'All those trains passing non-stop . . . The barges floating past every five minutes, one plane after the other, and all the traffic on the roads. Good Lord, I wonder why everybody's travelling around all the time. What do they have to do that's so urgent? Do *you* know, pal?'

'No.'

His expression was gloomy. Back when he was a cabbie,

he'd enjoyed observing his passengers, imagining their lives and their reasons for travelling. Each year on my birthday he'd let me ride in his taxi with the sign lit up.

'Are you free?' someone would always end up asking.

'Yes. Are you?' he'd answer.

This retort would throw the traveller into a lasting state of confusion. During the journey he and I would speculate about the customer who'd just got in with sneaky glances. Where had he just come from? From his mistress's flat? And what did this person do for a living? Undertaker? Umbrella salesman? How could we find out?

The broken meter was stuck on 0000, so Napoleon made up the prices off the top of his head. The customers never argued, and all the takings were mine to pocket.

'For your birthday!'

The meter had worked once – a long time ago – but the ticking drove him mad. He didn't like the idea of measuring time or distance.

'One day I punched it with a fist like Thor's hammer. You should have seen it – not a peep after that. Never let a meter push you around. Bust every one, or they'll suck the life out of you.'

His sole regret was that he'd never had a dog like Endov riding with him in the passenger seat. Incidentally, he began to miss Endov in hospital.

'That's just how it is,' my father told him. 'There's no point getting worked up. Dogs aren't allowed to visit.'

'They should ban wet blankets instead!' he whispered under his breath.

'What did he say?' my father asked.

'Oh, nothing,' I replied. 'He just said, "Never mind".'

The next day I brought along the drawings my mother had done of Endov to lift my grandfather's spirits. The dog was posing in profile. He seemed to be smiling. It was so lifelike that you could have sworn that Endov would bark at any moment and his whiskers would start to quiver.

'Thank God you're here, pal. It looks as if Endov is going to wag his tail, don't you reckon? Want to know something? Your father doesn't deserve her.'

'Who?'

'Your mum. If I'd had a daughter, I'd have loved her to have been like your mother. First of all, she doesn't talk much, which is a rare and significant quality in a woman. And then her drawings . . . You've no need for words when you can draw like that. We all talk too much, actually, and she's realised that.'

After a few more days, drawings were no longer enough. He wanted to see the dog.

'Even from afar. Please, you're my only hope. That's right – my only hope and my sole ally.'

So I got into the habit of bringing Endov and walking him in the hospital car park. Alexandre Rawcziik came along with me. One particular day he was messing around, putting his baseball cap on the dog's head, and it was the first time I'd ever heard him crack up laughing – a loud belly laugh that rang out into the sky.

Napoleon was able to look down at the dog's movements from his window. Endov soon grew tired of the drab surroundings. He always seemed to be looking around for his master. And every time a car drove up, he would lie down on his side.

After ten days or so Napoleon was transferred to a wheelchair. The cloud of misery that had hung over him since his arrival gave way to the spirit of rebellion. He circled his room like a caged lion, complaining about everything from the food to the TV programmes. Absolutely everything.

'It smells of underpants in here, pal! And the junior doctor has a dog's foul breath. I've never smelled anything like it. It's as if he farts every time he smiles. He should enter a talent contest! And as for the TV programmes, there's no doubt about it, they've tuned me into a special channel that makes you die of boredom. No westerns, no boxing matches, not a single motor or naked sexy lady. Eff all! All they talk about is the economic crisis and the stock market! It's TV for wet blankets!'

According to Napoleon, the hospital was keeping him there under duress and on my father's orders.

'They're going to put me down early, pal,' he sighed. 'In fact, they've already started. You know what? They've put me on a diet!'

'The gits!' I cried.

'No more sausages – can you believe that? And all because of a few scrapes.'

'A fracture, Grandpa. Of your vertebra.'

'Same difference. I'm telling you. They're locking me up! Your father's stalling for time so he can find an old people's home. I'm sure he's got a stack of brochures, arranged in order from the cheapest to the most expensive. If they really wanted to cure me, they wouldn't deprive me of sausages.'

He loved those little orange cocktail sausages you buy in strings. He flashed me an endearing wink.

'Maybe you can do something about that? A humanitarian gesture, you know. A dozen sausages.'

'OK, it's a deal. But in the meantime, you're seriously ill. You've got to save your energy.'

'You think Rocky saved his energy? Or gave up boxing and let something as banal as a back injury knock him down? No way. He fought until the bitter end. Like this – boom, boom!'

I realised during his stay that he'd known Rocky a lot better than he'd let on up to that point. They'd even been room-mates during the war when Napoleon was stranded on the other side of the Atlantic. They'd shared a bunk bed. It was funny to imagine them lying there, one above the other.

Rocky's parents had arrived in America from Italy ten

years before his birth. They had been born into misery, lived in misery and eventually died in misery. Their sole joy in life had been their son, and their sole victory had been over the pneumonia that had very nearly accounted for Rocky at the age of one.

Napoleon thought that Rocky had drawn his inexhaustible desire to win from the memory of his parents' wretched circumstances and the illness that had almost killed him. It was as if his life had been one long bid for revenge.

'It was poverty and that disease that made Rocky. His real name was Roberto.'

One day, summing up what bound him to Rocky, he murmured, 'Everything one boxer can give to another, Rocky gave to me.'

I didn't really dare ask what he meant by this, but the same idea crossed my mind: everything a grandfather can give to his grandson, Napoleon was giving to me. As if he could read my thoughts, he said, 'Thanks, pal. I don't know what I'd do without you! I don't know what would become of the empire. Hey, turn on the transistor – time for a little education. It won't do us any harm.'

The presenter's voice reached our ears clearly, distinctly, soothingly. The same encouraging voice would probably be asking the same questions a thousand years from now. I kept an eye on Napoleon's reaction. His smile was somewhat non-committal.

'A more challenging question now: what age did Victor Hugo live to?'

We heard the contestants whispering among themselves without being able to agree on an answer.

The presenter gave them a hint. 'Dear old Victor had a nice long life . . . '

'Seventy-five!' one of the contestants suggested.

'That's what that moron calls a long life?' raged Napoleon.

'Incorrect. The answer is eighty-three. Victor Hugo lived to be a very old man.'

The audience clapped.

'Turn it off!' Napoleon roared. 'A very old man! A mere kid, he was! He must have been frail. That presenter deserves a good kick up the arse. A little trip would've done him a world of good. He's so stuffy.'

The door was opened by a nurse pushing a little trolley laden with plasters, bandages, a thermometer and other medical equipment.

'Time for your treatment!' she trumpeted.

'Treatment, indeed!' grumbled Napoleon. 'She's going to try some of that suppository business again.'

He headed for the toilet in his wheelchair.

'Where are you going?' the nurse asked.

'For a piss. Or is that forbidden too?'

No sooner had he returned to his previous position than he declared, 'I'm warning you: my aide-de-camp isn't leaving the room. So if you had any plans to poison me on the sly, you can forget them.'

The nurse shrugged and prepared pills of every colour, which she then presented to him along with a glass of water and a smile. Then, making the most of his momentary lapse in concentration, she stuck the thermometer in his mouth.

'It doesn't usually go in the mouth,' she whispered to me, 'but at least this shuts him up for a couple of minutes. Your grandfather just can't keep still. He definitely lives up to his name.'

Napoleon glared and rolled his eyes.

The young woman eventually took out the thermometer and examined it. 'Forty-one degrees! How odd. He seems to be on top form.'

'I'm glad to hear you say so, miss.' Turning to me, he added, whispering, 'This nurse isn't bad, eh?'

'What did he say?' the young woman asked.

'Oh nothing – only that you're very kind.'

As the nurse was remaking the bed, Napoleon signalled to me to come closer.

'Help me out, pal, my eyes are a little sore. Can you tell me what it says on the nurse's scrubs. There. You see it?'

'On her scrubs?'

'Yes, above her right breast.'

'It says "Geriatrics", Grandpa.'

His eyes immediately went dead. It looked as if they'd

been replaced with marbles. He paled and his mouth became a thin, sharp line.

'Bloody hell. Are you sure?'

I nodded.

'What's wrong, Grandpa?'

'Don't call me that. Especially not now.'

Hurricane alert. His gaze, as keen as a knife blade, was riveted to the nurse's scrubs.

'Miss!' he yelled.

'Yes, sir?' said the startled nurse.

'What does it say there?'

His finger came to rest on the young woman's scrubs, and she recoiled.

'Here?'

'Yes, there. Are you deaf as well?'

I wondered whether Napoleon wasn't losing it a bit. The nurse took a while to reply.

'I'm waiting,' said Napoleon. 'In fact, that's all I do. But I'm warning you – there are limits to my patience.'

'As I'm sure you can see, it says "Geriatrics".'

My grandfather crossed his arms. His face was as impassive as stone.

'I can read, thank you.'

'It's my department. I work in the Geriatrics Unit, and so it says "Geriatrics".' Her voice sounded apologetic.

'Well, in that case, miss, you're going to do me a favour and find me a dictionary.'

'A dictionary? Oh, I see. For Scrabble. The pre-recorded final?'

'No, miss, for a hearty meal. What do you think? The live broadcast of *I Stop Taking The Piss Or I'm Going To Regret It*.'

Without needing to get to the bottom of what she'd done wrong, the nurse left the room.

'You see,' said Napoleon, 'I've got nothing against her personally, but some things need to be set straight. Made clear. Without delay. Everyone feels better afterwards.'

Ten minutes later the nurse handed Napoleon the dictionary he'd requested.

'I borrowed it from the man in the next room, who uses it for *Countdown*.'

Napoleon gave me a surreptitious look.

He spun one wheel of his chair to take him closer to the nurse.

'I don't want to know about your life, miss, or my neighbours'. I couldn't give a damn. Look up "geriatrics" yourself.'

She flicked through the pages, the tip of her tongue poking out between her teeth.

'Geriatrics . . . Geriatrics . . . Here it is!'

'Read it out – unless you don't know how to do that either!'

'All right then. "The branch of medical science that deals with the health and welfare of old people."' She looked up and smiled innocently. 'Did you know it comes from the Greek? Interesting, eh? It's incredible what you can learn. Are you happy now?'

Napoleon sank his nails into the arms of his wheelchair. A maze of veins stood out at his temples.

'You know what would really make me happy? To know what the bloody hell I'm doing in this department for the elderly!'

The nurse no longer knew how to cope with this nearly eighty-six-year-old pirate who was threatening to send everything flying.

He shouted, 'Yes, miss. I'd like to know what the hell I'm doing here with a load of old farts! I'm not asking for the moon, only for you to admit your mistake. THAT'S ALL!'

The nurse left the room in a hurry. Outside the window the declining sun was setting the surrounding countryside ablaze. My emperor appeared to have forgotten me as he sat there in his wheelchair, throwing air punches. It looked as if he was fighting against the dying of the light over the great plains of his empire.

12

About a fortnight later the head of department summoned my father. The doctor was worried. He didn't beat about the bush, obviously judging that it was better to tell it like it was.

'I'm going to be straight with you, Monsieur Sunshine: we cannot keep him here one minute longer. My entire staff are at the end of their tether and soon they'll be committing *us* to a mental institution.'

He told us the whole story, and I hung on every word.

Napoleon played ten-pin bowling in the corridors, using oxygen bottles for skittles, paid visits to other patients to challenge them to arm-wrestling bouts, made lewd comments whenever a nurse walked into his room and had recently started to grab them inappropriately.

'And the worst thing – the very worst of all – is that he destroys anything with a meter. He resets them to zero, shouting, "Bastards!". Last night all the fuses blew, and we couldn't work out why!'

Napoleon was in the eye of this storm of outrage and complaint.

'Yesterday he wheeled into the operating theatre, shouting, "Wait, wait you can't start without me!"'

'You think that's funny, do you?' Dad asked me when he caught sight of me trying to suppress a smile.

'You do have to admit it's . . . surprising,' my mother said, stifling a giggle, her eyes twinkling with delight. She put her hand on my knee.

'I have to say,' said my father, 'that I do not find it particularly amusing.'

'Sometimes even I have to contro—' the doctor continued. '. . . Um, I'm sorry, I'm talking gibberish. I'm tired. But he's going to cause some real damage if he carries on with this! Are you sure someone didn't get his date of birth wrong? By ten or twenty years, perhaps?'

'Absolutely not,' said my father.

'Because he really is remarkably robust. Abnormally robust. As a general rule, from the age of eighty onwards, and particularly after an accident like this that leaves the patient in a wheelchair, they begin to let themselves go. They put their affairs in order, but with him . . . Have you heard the latest?'

'N—no,' my father stammered.

'Well, hold on to your hat: he's talked about buying a motorbike.'

My father's mouth slowly fell open. 'A motorbike?'

'That's right. He said that if he has to get around on two wheels anyway ... He can't decide between a 650 and an 800 cc. He says that anything less than 500 cc is for ...'

'Wet blankets?' my father ventured.

'Yes.'

In any case, a solution had to be found. Napoleon was a handful. And so, in a Chinese restaurant near the hospital, my parents discussed the future of the emperor and his empire.

'There aren't very many solutions,' my father said, picking up a dumpling with his chopsticks. 'I've one in mind, but he's going to take it badly.'

'You mean a ho—'

'Yes, a home for o—'

My mother's lips twisted into a grimace. 'I can't really imagine him in a place like that. Can you see yourself saying, "I've got some news for you, Dad. You're going into an old pe—"'

'It's true. Oh, stop it, the mere thought ...' My father's fingers froze, and the dumpling slipped from his chopsticks and rolled under the table.

'It's a pity, actually,' my father went on, 'because he'd like it there. You know the place? The house opposite the school. It's pretty and peaceful.'

My mother answered him with a smile. *Pretty, peaceful*: the words were a little too restrictive for my grandfather.

It seemed Napoleon had been right all along. He had correctly anticipated his opponent's next moves.

'So that's it?' I said. 'You want to deport him!'

My father started, accidentally ramming a chopstick up his right nostril. He'd cut himself and started to bleed. He clamped his napkin to his nose.

'Deport him? Don't be ridiculous! We don't want to deport him – we want to make sure he gets proper care in a specialist institution with staff who can look after him and keep him entertained. It's worth saying that this is going to cost me a fortune!'

As if to vent his rage, he nervously stuffed a dumpling in his mouth and started to chomp frantically on it, producing a disgusting squishy sound, his napkin still held up to his nose. Then he stopped and stared at me for a few seconds without moving.

In a far milder tone of voice, he said, 'Leonard, do you know what it means to deport someone?' He looked me squarely in the eye, and I was unable to break away from his gaze.

'Well . . . actually . . . ' It was a word I'd heard Napoleon use.

My father sighed and squashed his napkin into a ball. He and my mother exchanged glances.

'Deporting someone, my love,' she said, 'is forcing someone to leave their home and even their town and then locking them up.'

'See,' my father said. 'It isn't the same thing at all.'

'And then what happens to them?' I asked.

'The person loses their rights. All their belongings are taken away. They're kept a long, long way from their loved ones, and quite often they never see them again.'

Alexandre's face fleetingly crossed my mind.

'And why do they do that?' I asked. 'Why?'

'Why?' My mother told me about the war and the trains that once crisscrossed Europe, carrying all the people who would never return home.

Her words faded as soon as she'd spoken them, and I couldn't remember everything she'd said. But I had the impression that the sentence 'They're kept a long, long way from their loved ones' would be engraved on my mind for ever, as if in stone.

The waiter approached us with a small utensil which he ran across the tablecloth to scoop up the crumbs.

'See that, darling? Very practical,' my father mumbled, suddenly amused.

Once the waiter had gone, my mother leaned towards my father.

'What if he simply stayed with us for a few weeks?' she suggested timidly.

'With us?' my father asked with a frown. 'You think that's a good idea?' His eyes betrayed his wariness.

'Only until he recovers,' my mother insisted. 'And, darling, it might give you both a chance to bury the hatchet.'

'He's the one who refuses to bury the hatchet. That trick

of his with the tie still makes me so angry. He can keep his bloody hatchet.' He pointed at his throat as he said this. There was suddenly something childish about his expression. 'You know the truth of the matter. He's never liked me. What can I do if I've never liked punching people, let alone getting my nose broken every weekend?'

He started pushing two wimpy fists out in front of himself.

'That's the only thing that would have endeared me to him. Pow! Pow! Becoming a boxer. And that isn't likely to change. Ever.'

My mother laid her hand on top of my father's and said very simply, 'The past is in the past. Napoleon won't live for ever.'

A letter from Grandma

My darling boy,

So, where was I? Oh yes, that Tuesday magazine, my niece who was passing through and who's gone off to Madrid to study Danish thought it was a good idea to give me a bit of a jolt, but according to her I should be careful. She said, 'You don't know who you're going to come across, what if it's some pervert who wants to slice you up, eh?'

The thing is though, I was being so careful I couldn't make up my mind, and then there were so many of them that they all began to seem alike. It's like when you want to buy a car, you never know whether to get the basic model that's reliable and never breaks down, or the model with lots of extras which is more tricky.

Well, I chose three different models and put them in order of preference, like horses on a betting slip, I wrote letters to all three (exactly the same, changing only the name), the first came back with the words 'No longer at this address' stamped on it, the second didn't give a damn, he never answered in fact, but I found a reply from the third in my letterbox a week later.

I met the gentleman, you can't imagine the butterflies in my tummy. He invited me to a Chinese restaurant, we ate all these things rolled up and wrapped up all razzmatazz and at the end they brought us these steaming white towels, sort of looked like pancakes, I bit into one and Edouard (that's the gentleman's name) burst out laughing, it wasn't a pancake, it was a moist towel. To wipe your hands, Edouard told me, he couldn't stop laughing and he told me it made him feel so good, he'd forgotten how it felt to laugh like that. According to him it was a sign that I'm the right model, I'd say.

The good thing is that I soon realised he didn't want to slice me up, so we went for a walk and I discovered that he'd owned an ironmonger's store before he retired. When I told him that I wasn't a widow as he believed but that my 85-year-old boxer husband had kicked me out to start afresh, at first he thought it was a joke, I'm supposed to see the gentleman again next week, he's going to take me to a Japanese restaurant. Anyway with his dumb ideas about widows he put grim thoughts in my head so I started knitting a jumper for your grandfather, I know you love him a lot so take good care of him and his new life, but don't you dare tell him I wrote or it will upset his newfound youth. Youths are delicate at 20 years old, so it can't be all that easy at 85.

Thinking of you,

Your grandma

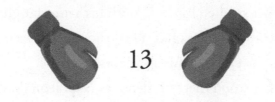

13

'With you?' asked Napoleon, his voice devoid of emotion. 'Did I hear you correctly? Or am I going deaf? Now? At my age?'

My father was standing opposite him.

'That's right – with us.'

'And you came up with this idea all by yourself?' asked Napoleon. 'Or did you pick it out in a lucky dip?'

'Just until you get your spirits back, you know.'

'I'll tell you if I need you to look after my spirits, thank you very much. So if you could just please mind your own business . . .'

Napoleon stared down at the floor by his feet. He was smiling.

'Oh, by the way, while I think of it, there's one thing that's always annoyed me about you.' Napoleon looked down at my father's feet.

'Just the one?'

'No, but this one more than any other right now. It's that you wear square-toed shoes.'

My father studied his feet. With his arms dangling by his sides, he really did look like a little boy who's been told that he has forgotten to tie his shoelaces.

My father stood there in silence as Napoleon doubled over with laughter. Dad merely walked over to the window and plunged his hands into his trouser pockets. The reflection of his face in the glass blended with the hilly countryside beyond it.

Suddenly Napoleon moved his wheelchair to position himself beside my father. The two men watched a plane on its approach for landing. From my vantage point on the edge of the bed I could see them both from behind: Napoleon hunched in his wheelchair and my father perched on the tips of his square-toed shoes, striving to reach some imaginary bar. They looked even more different from each other from the back than they did from the front.

'Strange, eh?' Napoleon muttered. 'All these people travelling all the time.'

'It is, yes,' my father said. 'It is strange.'

I was sure that my mother would have been able to catch in a drawing those few seconds of closeness between them.

'Hey!' my father exclaimed. 'I've got another idea. A home nur— ... I mean, a female companion.'

Napoleon said nothing for several seconds, apparently

waiting for a plane to disappear into the clouds high above, then mumbled, 'Is she pretty?'

Irene's references were rock solid. She was a member of some kind of specialist unit for supervising unstable people, most of them elderly, and she practised various martial arts including judo, ju-jitsu, karate, tae kwon do, Thai boxing, Krav Maga and Japanese foot-fighting, as well as yoga. She was therefore an expert in controlling others, and in self-control.

'No one has made me lose my cool yet,' she said the day she visited us. 'I wear even the toughest ones down in the end. With me they return to the great sea of serenity because I am inhabited by the spirit of the ... SHOGUN.'

Her head was drawn in between her shoulders and she resembled a hedgehog when she was in a good mood and a bulldog when she bared her fangs. She could look twenty or fifty, depending.

'Be careful, though,' my father told her. 'You're taking on a heavyweight this time! Don't forget that he's called Napoleon. It's a sign.'

'I'll manage,' Irene declared.

'All we ask is that you get him to accept that an almost eighty-six-year-old needs some help and can no longer live on his own ... If you could only get it into his thick skull that he's old – very old and not immortal.'

Irene seemed very composed. Mum had taken a seat in

a corner of the living room and was wielding her pencils so fast that they were almost invisible.

'Consider it done,' said Irene. 'In a month's time he'll be begging you to put him in an old people's home. I use the ancient technique of the Japanese shoguns: I isolate, envelop and smother!'

'Be careful all the same. He can throw serious punches!'

'That may well be true,' she said, 'but you have to trust me.'

'Wow, you really do have a special way of looking at people. I feel quite blessed that you're here.'

'I'd like to begin straight away and, don't forget, no visits until I give the green light, because with the shogun spirit, I isolate, envelop and smother! Like this.'

She throttled an invisible prey with her bare hands.

For over a fortnight I heard nothing from my grandfather. Every time I called I got Irene. She let me speak, but all she said was, 'I'll pass on the message.'

Irene was in full-isolation mode. Her neutral voice betrayed no trace of feeling or emotion.

'And, um, is he all right?'

'We're on the road together.'

'The road?'

'The road to the great sea of serenity, the boundless ocean of wisdom. The navel of the shogun is shining on us!'

Occasionally I would walk past his house and, through

the curtains, make out the vague outline of Irene moving his wheelchair. Or I would guess that they were sitting opposite each other at the table.

Irene was all-enveloping.

Autumn arrived. We had to put back the clocks, and the light faded earlier every evening. Dad ticked off the days on a calendar. Each completed day filled him with hope, and brochures for old people's homes piled up on the coffee table in our living room. It was my father's hope that Irene was only a short-term solution.

The weather was cold, grey and miserable. I missed my emperor. Endov also missed him, because Irene had refused to look after him, probably with the intention of breaking down my grandfather and knocking some sense into him. The dog was sad too and watched through the window for his master's return. When night fell, Endov would whimper as if realising that he'd have to wait some time before he would see Napoleon again. Whenever he heard a car engine, he played dead. Great actors sometimes find it hard to quit the stage.

I often took him for walks with Alexandre. Even if sometimes I wasn't sure who was walking whom, I always felt as if an invisible leash bound us together. We were three poor soldiers in full retreat. Not once did Alexandre remove his strange headgear, which actually looked more like a carnival hat or a Cossack's headdress than a cap.

Alexandre would sometimes vanish for an entire after-noon, leaving his seat in class empty. Where did he go? He never gave any explanation for these absences. Respecting the tacit agreement that had governed our relationship from the beginning, I always took pains to hide my curiosity, but our classmates had no compunction about bombarding him with questions. His invariable silence unleashed storms of disdain and distrust, and the most outrageous rumours were propagated about him.

He would return from each of his escapades with small objects that he took care to keep concealed from the others, but which he was kind enough to show me. There were delicate red-and-gold badges, football stickers and various other mysterious trinkets.

One evening I complimented him. 'Your key ring's nice!' I said. 'I'd love to have one like that. You're so lucky.'

'Maybe I am lucky,' he mumbled.

I couldn't work out exactly what it was that drew me to Alexandre Rawcziik. Was it his outlandish cap, which he guarded as if it were treasure? His strange silences? His strange passion for insects? Or simply his curiosity about Napoleon's adventures? Alexandre waited to hear about them as you might anticipate the next episode of a soap opera, one that you hope will never end. I felt that he alone could truly appreciate the stories and that the two of us together were powerful enough to prevent them from being forgotten.

I did indeed tell him one tale after another about the fights of yesteryear, the screaming spectators, the lonely changing rooms and the rigged bouts. I took him on imaginary tours of Brooklyn gyms and initiated him into the boxer's arsenal of tricks. I embroidered, I embellished, I adorned. For his pleasure I fabricated Napoleon's life with Rocky during his American exile. I also told Alexandre that there was no need to worry, for Napoleon would find the chink in the nurse's armour and come back to us stronger than ever.

Each time Alexandre removed another marble from his pocket.

'That was a good story. Have a marble.'

I spent a lot of time at home. One Sunday evening my mother showed me an album full of scenes from our family life that she had drawn over the years. Sometimes she would sketch them on the spot; at others she would let her memory guide the pencil.

'Do you remember this?' she asked me.

It was the moment Dad received the tie Napoleon had given him. The drawing showed Dad holding it proudly aloft. His expression was joyful, like a child unwrapping a Christmas present. Had Mum exaggerated the happiness burning inside him?

'And this one was the next day, just after his lecture! A completely different atmosphere!'

Dad was angrily waving the tie as my grandfather erupted

with laughter. You could almost feel my father's rage and hear my emperor's roar of delight.

As I studied these drawings, I was struck by a terrifying realisation: Napoleon had aged. His skin, which my mother had observed with such subtlety, was wrinkled and lines now furrowed his face. His shoulders, which had once been so broad, were more now stooped, and his twinkling, menacing eyes had dulled from one page to another. Time, which seemed to stand still in the real world, flowed past relentlessly on paper. However immortal and invincible he might seem to me in the flesh, in the drawings he was becoming increasingly fragile and ephemeral.

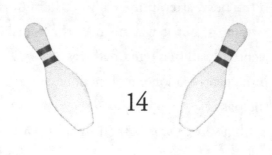

14

Every Saturday in the few weeks that saw autumn turn to winter, Irene dropped a meticulous report into our letterbox for my father.

Dad was ecstatic. Napoleon was sailing smoothly towards the shores of the great sea of serenity. I begrudged him his premature celebrations.

'She's just amazing! There's nothing like ancient wisdom, Lao Tzu and the whole caboodle, to hammer some sense into someone. Honestly, why go on fighting when you're eighty-five? You give up the struggle at that age. You behave yourself. That's the way of the world. You stop rebelling.'

Those words haunted me like vultures. I dreamed of a forest whose trees swayed for no reason. There was no wind, but the giant hardwoods shook and then eventually they fell, one after the other, like great dominoes, to deafening silence.

Endov, Alexandre Rawcziik and I were there, running from one tree to the next, attempting to hold them upright with our puny strength, but it was no use: they crashed to the ground. Eventually all that remained was a dreary plain and, standing in its centre, a lone, melancholy emperor with his mind on the past.

I woke with a start. I was bathed in cold sweat.

One Wednesday the phone rang. I had only just got out of bed and my mother was already drawing in her little den as if she'd been there all night. I picked up.

'I'd like to speak to my aide-de-camp.'

I felt my legs turn to jelly. My heart began to pound so hard that I thought it would jump right out of my chest.

'My emp'ror?' I said uncertainly.

'Who else. The army is routed, but the empire is saved!'

'Did you get rid of her?'

'Sure did, but she was a tough opponent. Fortunately, I had that trick from the final against Etchevaria up my sleeve. Remember the one?'

'Yeah, the "hook, line and sinker"!'

'Spot on! You pretend you no longer exist, you go all transparent and just when the other guy thinks you're finished – bang! You hit him with a last-minute torpedo.'

'You're the best! So the struggle goes on, eh?'

'You bet it does! As long as you struggle, you're alive. Come and get me – I need to get into shape.'

I ran to his house.

'Where is she?' I asked.

Napoleon was sitting in his wheelchair, pulling on his black jacket and his beanie with some difficulty. He pointed to the end of the corridor.

'In the toilet?' I cried. 'You locked her in the toilet?'

'Yeah. I know it's not the most original act of self-defence, but sometimes you have to accept that it's no holds barred if you want to save the match. Come on, pal, we have to go.'

'You're going to leave her in there?'

'She'll be fine. More time for her to reflect!'

She must have been listening because we heard her call out from the bathroom: 'A wise man never humiliates his adversary, Confucius said.'

Not missing a beat my grandfather replied, 'A philosopher can make do with even the smallest space.'

There was silence for a couple of seconds.

'Lao Tzu?' Irene asked in a hesitant voice.

'No – Napoleon!'

I managed to push him into the front seat of the Peugeot 404 without too much fuss. Before starting the engine he asked me, 'What about Endov? How's he doing?'

'He's keeping an eye on our rearguard.'

'Good. Excellent. The empire is safe with you two around.'

Napoleon's triumphant wheelchair entrance into the bowling alley took everyone by surprise, but the only comment was, 'Good to see you again, emperor. Your usual lane?'

He insisted on donning his elegant shoes. I hesitated, but, no, he was serious. His feet looked tiny in my hands.

'Tie them nice and tight, pal. Double-knot the laces.'

Now all we had to do was adapt to the circumstances. He'd explained everything to me in the car.

'Let's go, Joe.'

I pushed the wheelchair across the wooden floor. It barely moved, the wheels squealing on the varnished boards.

'Faster! Push harder, for God's sake!'

I ran, I fell over, scraping my knees, and then grabbed hold of the chair again. At last we got up to top speed. I stepped on the brakes and the wheelchair slid abruptly forward.

'Go, girl!' said Napoleon.

The pins scattered and my grandfather's laughter shattered the air. The automatic mechanism installed a completely new set of skittles. Tac-clack!

Between two strikes we went for a Coke at one of the low tables. He loved the fizzy drink because it reminded him of the States.

'I'm sick of this back pain!' he said.

'Don't worry, Grandpa. It'll click back into place.'

'Know what annoys me the most?' he asked.

I shook my head as I sucked Coke through a straw.

'That you're almost as tall as me now.'

I thumped him on the shoulder and stood beside the wheelchair.

'Taller, actually. Look!'

'It's a matter of debate You're standing on your tiptoes, so it doesn't count. And my tyres are flat. You remind me of your father, acting like a ballerina en pointe! In the meantime . . .' Planting his elbow on the table top, he wiggled his fingers in the air, summoning my hand. 'Chickening out, are you?'

'No way.'

Our hands joined. Our muscles tensed. Palm against palm as ever. Our eyes met. I resisted. No, I did more than just resist and I realised that my emperor wasn't putting it on. I caught a glimmer of worry in his eye, which he tried to disguise with a carefree smile. He was giving it his all, clenching his jaw, and I had more strength in reserve. Lots of strength. I only needed to give a tiny bit more to carry the day, but suddenly I was overcome with an intense sadness. Now it was my duty to pretend. I let go. My hand was flattened against the table as usual.

'Unbeatable,' I said.

There was an awkwardness between us.

'Promise me something, pal.'

'Anything.'

'That you'll never, ever, wear square-toed shoes.'

*

All around us, pins toppled and players let out shrieks of joy. Grandpa used his straw to suck up the remaining drops in the bottom of his glass. He frowned, then affected a relaxed air.

'Any news from your grandma?'

'None, Grandpa.'

'Don't call me that. For God's sake.'

A waitress came over to clear away our glasses, and Napoleon waited for her to leave before continuing.

'She's overdoing it!'

'*She's* overdoing it? You can talk!' I said.

'Yeah – vanishing like that!'

I wondered whether he was joking. But, no, he appeared to mean it. He ran an imperious eye over the bowling alley and the players sauntering up to the lanes before releasing their balls.

'See this, pal,' Napoleon said, pointing to his special bowling ball. It had 'Born to Win' written across it. He was cradling it in the crook of his elbow like a baby.

'Well, it's going to be yours. You'll take good care of it.'

Two days later Dad received a letter from Irene, the home nurse. Expecting anything but an unconditional surrender, he began to read it aloud in a confident voice.

'"Dear Sir, I can tell you that I have seen a lot of old people, but there are not many of your father's kind left . . . A unique case . . . Luckily, in fact, because if there were a whole host of them . . . "'

My father furrowed his brow and bit his lip. He skimmed the rest of the letter with a worried look, his voice growing fainter and his face turning pale as if all the blood were draining from it.

'"And that was nowhere near the worst of it, because just imagine the next day he appeared in my room and . . . "'

My father almost fainted. His legs began to give way beneath him, but he grabbed the table to stop himself from crumpling to the floor. Mum fanned him with the frying pan she was holding. Yet he still made an effort to continue his reading, although by now his voice was shaking. Mum read the letter over his shoulder.

'"So when I had recovered I told him that boxing gloves and rock 'n' roll were the opposite of the shogun's philosophy. I know, I shouldn't have – you have to understand that I was at my wits' end and I had abandoned wisdom – but I ended up calling him a crazy old man. His response hit me like a missile to the gut. He said . . . "' My mother didn't dare read any further.

'What a nerve!' my father said.

Finally, Irene announced that she was leaving for the south of France. She didn't want to run into any more maniacs like my grandfather, who withstood everything you could throw at them. In her closing sentence she insisted that the only person she was angry with was herself, her sole regret being that Napoleon had been unable to make the most of shogun wisdom. She wished him a long life and assured us

113

that the shogun, in his goodness, would nevertheless take care of my grandfather – albeit from a distance.

Dad crumpled up the letter and kicked it across the room.

'Back to square one!' he said despondently. 'It's a good thing Josephine's out of the way, to be honest.'

A letter from Grandma

My darling boy,

Those Japanese really are very clever, but they
make things more complicated than I'd ever have
imagined, you see, on Saturday night Edouard took
me out to dinner at a Japanese restaurant because,
as you know, he is passionate about the culture, all
the dishes there end in the letter 'I', they served us
little bits of square fish, with nothing else, no sauce or
cream; no cutlery either, well, you know me, I sent it
all back to the kitchen because it really wasn't cooked
or seasoned, and I thought that in spite of their polite
and smiley manner, they were taking the mickey.

Edouard explained that this was an ancient and
refined culinary tradition that took some getting
used to and had to be learned, I said fine, but I didn't
get it, a thousand years and all they came up with was
raw fish ...

What with the hot towels that looked like
pancakes the other day and yesterday's raw fish, not

to mention the chopsticks, which I thought were giant toothpicks, I wonder if this little man isn't pulling my leg in order to play the expert; halfway through dinner Edouard explained (he loves explaining) that his wife had gone two years ago due to something wrong with her lungs, I can't remember its name, I don't know what came over me (maybe the very spicy green stuff they put on the fish) but I asked him if she'd had a good journey, and tears welled up in his eyes and I couldn't stop laughing, it was silly but the more I tried to stop, the harder I laughed, and the harder I laughed the more his face crumpled, and seeing him all crumpled made me giggle, so to apologise I kissed him on the cheek and he blushed and it looked pretty, we didn't say anything for a while, it was embarrassing, I ended up saying I was sorry even though I wasn't really, I've noticed that you can get out of any situation by saying you're sorry (make a note of that).

Towards the end of the meal he asked if I liked board games, and I was pleased, especially because I was deprived of games my whole life with your grandfather, bridge, rummy and whist aren't really up his street, as you know, because of his short attention span, and he never wanted anything to do with Scrabble, saying it was a thing for wet blankets. Once he went with me to the seniors' club but he got all worked up for nothing and caused a scandal.

Anyway, that was a Brownie point for Edouard, the board games, we had a glass of sake in a glass with a picture at the bottom and I went all red because it was of a naked man with a huge willy, I didn't say anything because I didn't want to seem prudish, then Edouard asked me, 'Do you like Go?'

What on earth? I almost asked but I was fed up with asking questions, I was turning into a question mark, so I said yes, it's generally easier to say yes, say yes and they leave you in peace, make a note of that too. 'Go,' Edouard said, 'the game of Go, a Japanese game, Japanese chess if you prefer, I'll explain it to you one day, we're going to have great fun'. He talked to me as if I was seriously ill and I wondered who he thought he was, he was annoying me with his formal talk and his superior airs, educating me, you see the first difference between Edouard and Napoleon is that after five minutes in his taxi your grandfather was calling me by my first name, and Edouard is still calling me Madame Sunshine several weeks on.

We were wandering around the lake and I didn't know why but I really wanted to cry. I felt both lost without your grandfather and overflowing with him, as soon as I got home I went back to the piece of knitting I'd started. Edouard has promised to take me to a Korean restaurant next time, all he thinks about is eating, it's unbelievable, so I looked up where Korea was on a map, it's a long way away. See, darling, I'm travelling.

I hope you haven't said anything to Napoleon about my letters, I keep thinking about that night when I knocked on his taxi window and asked if he

was free, and I too was free, and by the next morning
neither of us was, I'd encountered happiness, you
see (I've never met anyone who lives up to his name
more than your grandfather), sometimes I think that
I'm going to weep for the rest of my days because of
Napoleon (what a brute he is!), and at other times
it's just the opposite, I feel as if he's always with me,
following me wherever I go, and I only need to turn
round and there he is smiling at me.

Your loving grandma

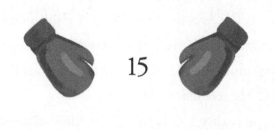

15

I was sure that life would go back to how it had been before. Exactly as it had been before. Just a little glitch, as my grand-father liked to say. He'd got back on his feet so many times that one more time wouldn't be so hard.

But the joy of our reunion quickly faded. The walls stripped of paper, the furniture still gathered in the middle of the room and the smell of damp in the air made me sad. A spectre of abandonment seemed to haunt the property. In one fell swoop, for the very first time, I had the feeling that reality was stronger than we were. Stronger than my emperor, stronger than the efforts of all mankind put together.

I was suddenly certain that we wouldn't manage and I was ashamed of that certainty, ashamed to find myself thinking like my father. Ashamed of growing up and sensing that my grandpa and I were no longer invincible.

'Hey, pal, not feeling well? We made pretty good progress, eh? The end is in sight, don't you think?'

'Yes, my emperor, the end is in sight.'

And so, as the days wore on, I took to hiding my discouragement. Occasionally Napoleon would fall into silence and despair, slumping back in his wheelchair and eventually dozing off. He seemed gutted.

To escape reality I shut myself in the bathroom. Was it my emperor who had turned the photo of Rocky around? There, with his face pressed to the wall, Rocky was well and truly dead.

I brought him back to life, and he looked at me again. Proud roars rose from chests once more. Fists landed muffled punches. Rocky wasn't fighting with a feather duster ... A piledriver of a hook ... Napoleon staggered but righted himself ... Rocky skipped about to wind him up. Napoleon fell into his trap and failed to execute his famous 'hook, line and sinker'. And yet there wasn't the slightest doubt that Napoleon was superior in every respect and Rocky looked in bad shape. This one wasn't going to get away. Then, straight after the break between rounds, the tables were turned ... Rocky adopted the perfect strategy ... A double-fisted charge ... My emperor was down ... The referee was counting, one ... two ... three ...

*

Some days my emperor would recover a semblance of drive, and he was almost his former self again. I made the most of these opportunities to bombard him with questions – as subtle and soft as a caress one moment, as direct as a straight right the next.

'What was your secret, my emperor?'

'My secret?'

'Your secret as a fighter.'

'Aha ...' His voice quivered vaguely with relief. 'Well, you see, pal, my tactics were very shrewd, very cunning. Try to keep them in mind.'

'I will.'

Endov came round and sat rigidly by my side, as if he was aware of the importance of these imminent revelations.

'So ... at the beginning of the fight I would punch as hard as I could. Like this.' It looked as if pistons were firing his fists out in front of him.

'In the middle of the fight I punched as hard as I could.'

'And at the end?' I asked innocently.

'At the end? I punched as hard as I could. How else? Like this!' His fist slammed into the wall, and the wheelchair was thrown backwards before spinning in a circle.

'Is your fist OK?' I asked.

'Yeah, why?'

'Because the wall isn't too happy. Look.'

A crack had appeared, zigzagging diagonally up the wall, and some plaster had dropped onto the floor.

His last fight against Rocky haunted me. The more time passed, the more I was filled with a creeping certainty that the bout had not been rigged and that Napoleon hadn't fought to the end as he ought to have done. Something had happened, but what? The mystery was burning inside me and one day I blurted out my question.

'Oh, my emperor, why didn't you fight to the end?'

'What did you say, pal?'

Without waiting for my answer he turned on the radio.

'It's *Who Wants To Win A Thousand Euros?*' he said. 'Thank God for this guy. Makes a change from all the circling vultures and wet blankets. Shh, it's about to start!'

'I'm not the one who can't stop talking, it's you.'

'Shush. Listen, for God's sake. That's brilliant! Reminds me of a boxer who went on and on in the ring, reeling off the story of his life. Blah blah blah and blah blah blah.'

'See, you're doing it again. Shh.'

'You shush.'

'A mathematical question. If one takes a figure and increases it by twenty-five per cent, by what percentage must one reduce the result to produce the original figure?'

Napoleon turned to me. 'Do you know?'

'No.'

'Twenty per cent,' the contestant answered.

'Yes, that's right.'

'Did you know that?'

'Not at all.'

The questions came thick and fast. How many stomachs does a cow have? Which year was Sarah Bernhardt born? How many recycled plastic bottles does it take to make a jumper? Who invented inverted commas? (My grandfather replied 'me' and burst out laughing.) Why do we say 'hello' when we answer the phone?

'Well, we could say "shit", but it wouldn't go down so well,' Napoleon said, turning off the radio. 'It's amazing how knowledgeable people are! I can't get over it. I'd love to send in a question of my own one day.' Then he gave me a wink and said, 'It's easier to ask questions than to answer them, eh?'

'Shall we get back to work?' I asked.

He studied the bare walls in surprise, as if seeing them for the first time.

'What a mess' was all he said. 'I wonder if there's any point in all this. You see, pal, we do things and a short time later we don't know why we do them.'

'You wanted to start a new life, remember. Have you changed your mind?'

'Of course I haven't. But maybe the age of conquest is coming to an end. Don't worry, though – we'll defend our borders and save our lands!' He brandished his fist. 'Tooth and nail!'

Particles of dust seemed to be suspended in the fading light. The house was gradually eaten up by shadows. He stroked Endov's head for some time, and then began to talk about memories of his life in America. The subterranean jazz clubs. Broadway in the wee small hours of the morning with Rocky. I could hear their footsteps on the tarmac. The powerful Harley he rode.

'The Yanks bug you less about having a driving licence. You buy a stamp and you ride away. And you might as well use your helmet as a chamber pot.'

The day Gary Cooper came to see him box.

'Well, not me, really, but he did shake my hand in the changing room. You have heard of Gary Cooper, haven't you?'

I shook my head. He banged the arm of his wheelchair.

'Bloody hell, this is unbelievable. He hasn't heard of Gary Cooper! No wonder the world's going to the dogs.'

He looked seriously outraged. I stopped myself from saying that no one of my age had heard of Gary Cooper. It was a question of different generations. His fingers made two little revolvers, which he aimed at me.

'Get ready to die, Bill,' he said in a booming voice.

'Spare me,' I pleaded.

'No, Bill, this world ain't big enough for the both of us. It's either you or me, and I've decided it's going to be me. Because I'm on the right end of this Colt.'

He made the sound of a gun being fired and I crumpled to the floor. He blew on the smoking barrels of his imaginary pistols.

'That was Gary Cooper, pal. A cowboy. *The* cowboy. Not

like all the wet blankets around nowadays. You can't tell whether actors today are boys or girls!'

At last he fell silent for a few seconds. He stifled a series of little burps.

'You've got to give me a hand, pal,' he said.

'With what?'

He hesitated. 'I'm tired.'

Tired? How strange to hear that word coming from his mouth. He seemed to want to correct himself.

'Don't go getting any big ideas! I'm just feeling a little ill. I've got a bit of a tummy ache. I opened a tin of sardines that had been hanging around for a while and now they're swimming back upstream. The tin was a bit rusty – and so were those little tiddlers.'

I rummaged in the bin. The tin dated from before tins were invented.

'Was it a present from Gary Cooper?'

He smiled. 'Don't breathe a word about this. Come on, help me to bed.'

He leaned on my shoulder to haul himself into his bed. He was as light as a butterfly. I drew the sheet and the covers up to his frail chin. It was weird: for the first time I felt as if I was taking care of him. I brought my face close to his head. His hair was silky, if a little sparse.

'How about letting Josephine know, my emperor? Don't you want to see her again?'

'Has she written to you?'

I hesitated. 'No.'

'You know, pal, there's one thing I haven't told you.'

'About the match against Rocky?'

He remained silent for a few seconds, and I wondered if he might have fallen asleep.

'No,' he said. 'About Josephine. You know I told you about the night she got into my taxi?'

'Yes, I do.'

'She said, "Just drive and we'll see where we get to." We came to this beach in Normandy, a place called ... Oh, I don't know any more. She'll remember; she remembers everything. She remembers for both of us.'

I gave him a peck on the cheek. His skin was soft. The air was freezing, and the tears running down my face turned to little streams of ice.

In my dreams the trees continued to fall, one after the other, in total silence. I would often wake before dawn, bathed in sweat.

In the middle of one of those nights the phone rang. My father got up. I have no idea what time it might have been or whether it was closer to the evening before than to the morning after. I tried to guess who might be on the other end of the line, but my father barely answered, or maybe he did but very quietly, and I had trouble understanding what he said. Was my emperor calling him for help?

A few minutes later the front door slammed and the car

started. It wasn't a reassuring sound, but more as if fate had come knocking.

The next morning I took advantage of breakfast to ask my mother, 'I have a feeling the phone rang last night, Mum.'

'One of your dad's employees had a car accident.'

'But Dad drove off, didn't he?'

'Yes. To . . . fetch some important files the employee had taken with him.'

Her face was as white as her lie. I left for school, my jaw numb with anxiety. The worst kinds of visions flashed through my head.

Alexandre noticed. He was wearing his cap perched high on his head, its leather strap gleaming in the sun. I had genuinely never seen anyone else wear this kind of headgear.

He wanted me to tell him a story, but I couldn't. Even the noise of marbles clicking together in his pocket in an attempt to unlock my resistance didn't work. He smiled and whispered, 'Some things cannot be spoken, and such things are sacred.'

At that moment I felt as if silence could create a stronger bond than any words could.

At the beginning of the next break, some boys stole Alexandre's cap as he passed the coat pegs. Clutching their spoils, they immediately rushed out into the playground, screeching like Sioux warriors. Alexandre was as stunned as if he'd been scalped and all he could say was, 'I was sure this would happen one day.'

The incredible cap was tossed from hand to hand like a rugby ball and then kicked around in the playground dust. When the boys wearied of this game, they took to stamping on the cap to finish it off.

'Hang on,' I said. 'Watch this.'

'Oh, leave it!' he said as he tried to hold me back.

But I was already on the warpath. I could feel Napoleon's long legacy coursing through my veins. I knocked out three in quick succession, and the others thought it best to turn their attention to something other than the cap – or what was left of it, to be more precise.

Alexandre Rawcziik gazed at it with tears in his eyes. He examined it from all sides and tried to mould it back into shape, but it was now no more than a scrap of fabric whose garish colours were obscured by layers of ground-in dust. His chin was wobbling. He stretched out his hand and in his palm were the remaining marbles, 'Here you are. You've more than earned them. Never stake them again.'

'Keep them for a little longer if you'd like.'

He gave them to me, smiled and held up the multi-coloured rag that had once been his faithful friend.

'See this? It's only fit for the bin.'

'No, no. We're going to my grandma's in the south of France over the Christmas holidays. I'm sure she'll be able to mend it for you. Here, give it to me.'

He hesitated for a second before handing it over. I could tell from the look in his eye that this cap was as sacred to him as my marbles were to me. I returned the marbles to him and said, 'Here, keep them until I bring your hat back. I'm sure my mum lied to me. Something's happened to Napoleon.'

On the way home from school Alexandre and I stopped off at a phone box and dialled Napoleon's number. There was no answer, nothing but a dozen hollow rings. So we parted with barely another word.

But, perhaps because I was now responsible for his cap or because I was feeling anxious, I decided to stay close to Alexandre and follow him home. I thought I'd do it for a short time for comfort. I didn't want to go home. I was too scared. He walked slowly, his hands deep in his pockets and his shoulders hunched forward, lost in thought. The bag of marbles tied to his belt slapped against his thigh with every step. I realised that he was walking maybe not completely aimlessly, but taking some sort of scenic route instead. He sought out the most remote lanes, the most unlikely routes and sometimes took the same path several times. For a split second I wondered if he wasn't trying to throw someone off the scent.

He would occasionally stop abruptly, and apparently in deep concentration, take a small length of wood from his pocket. I realised that Alexandre was transferring the insects he came across to safe places – under a bench or against a wall, wherever they weren't likely to be crushed by a passer-by. I suddenly felt ashamed of having tailed him and took the very next turning.

With concern for my grandfather's health preying on my mind, I decided to face it and go home, determined to challenge my mother. But she wasn't there. I shut myself in my room, feeling about as battered as Alexandre's cap.

I heard the front door open. My parents came into the house, followed by a thin, distinguished-looking woman whose very brown hair was gathered into a tight bun held in place by two chopsticks. Everything about her was wiry, sharp and angular. The bun was her only rounded, gentle feature.

I quickly realised that she was the director of the old people's home, and I was surprised by the sense of relief this gave me. At least Napoleon was alive. I tiptoed out into the hallway and tried to spy on their conversation through the half-open door.

'I can assure you that your father will be in very good hands with us. We have highly qualified staff who are ready to deal with every imaginable situation.'

'He's not your typical old man. He's in a bad state but not in the least resigned. Let's just say that he is far more stubborn than your average person.'

Once again I had the strange impression of being caught up in one of my mother's drawings. I could see that her eyes were glued to the director's bun even as she listened to the conversation.

'Many people do indeed come to us reluctantly,' the woman said, 'but after a few weeks they feel at home and nothing in the world would make them leave. We take one of them, we spoil them and entertain them, and they come round to the idea that they should make the most of this enriching, albeit final stretch of life. They can even go swimming with Silvio, you know.'

'Silvio?' my father asked with a frown.

'Yes, the lifeguard. He makes sure that our residents' rebellion is gradually watered down.'

'Look here,' my father said, 'I'm not asking you to dissolve him in chlorine, only to protect him from himself.'

Pens scraping on paper: my father signed the contract with furious concentration. My mother's expression was inscrutable, emotionless. The woman snapped her briefcase shut. Like a guillotine coming down.

'Now for the hardest part,' said my father. 'Persuading him. I'm not doing this with a light heart, believe me.'

The lady interrupted my father with a hand on his shoulder. Her face softened into an unexpectedly gentle smile.

'It's a common situation, sir. You feel guilty.'

'You're not wrong,' my father said, standing up on the tips of his square-toed shoes.

'No time, very little space. Modern life. He'll be better off and safer in the home with us.'

My father's expression suddenly gave way to a dreamy mist that veiled his eyes. 'Who'd have imagined, eh?' he whispered. 'Obviously you didn't know him back in the day when—' He broke off. He looked at the floor, swallowed and stared straight into the director's eyes. '—when he was in his prime. The thought of my father in an old people's home! My God!'

'A *welcome* home, if you please. You'll see – give it a few weeks and you won't regret a thing.'

'If you say so. I simply don't see any other solution. He's losing his mind! He's had a screw loose for several weeks now. You have to admit that getting divorced at the age of eighty-five is a bit peculiar, but then there was the time we found him in the boot of his car. We never really figured out why. And last night topped the lot: the police called me from Chartres to say that a lorry driver had picked him up by the side of the road.'

'How on earth did he get there?' the lady exclaimed.

'I don't know. He must have hitchhiked. He couldn't recall a thing this morning. All he could say was "What are you doing here in your square-toed shoes?"'

The silence lasted several seconds. The director slowly lowered her gaze to the tips of my father's shoes. A smile formed on her lips.

'Would you like me to have a word with him?' she asked. 'To introduce him to his future friends?'

'No way! Only if you want all hell to break loose and you

132

feel like closing your home down for good. That's a terrible idea. No, I've got a better one. It's his birthday next week. We'll invite him round and if we manage things properly, maybe ...'

I silently returned to my room. I took out an atlas from my small bookshelf and looked up a map of France. Chartres wasn't far from Normandy.

Later that evening I rang Napoleon once again. This time he picked up the phone quickly and straight away, as if it couldn't possibly be anyone else on the end of the line, and said, 'Pal! I thought you'd got into trouble.'

Hearing his voice cheered me up immediately.

'Are you all right?'

'Tip-top. What could possibly go wrong? It's your father who's a little off his rocker at the moment. He turned up at my house this morning with a face six feet long.'

'Are you sitting down, Grandpa?'

'No, I'm standing on my head!'

'I have a message for my emperor.'

'Watch out – we might be under surveillance. Be wary of everything and everyone.'

'You were right. They want to deport you.'

This time he was silent for much longer. A sort of groan came down the phone line before he asked, 'Ready to resist?'

'At your command!'

A letter from Grandma

Darling Leonard,

Honestly, my dear boy, I've got myself into a pretty
pickle and I'm being polite. Edouard, who I've told
you about (you know, the one who eats a chop with
chopsticks), well he's got it into his head to show me
Japan and the whole of Asia, from north to south and
east to west, very nice of him, you'll say, but I prefer
Europe and actually Western Europe. As I told you
he knows that part of the world very well because
he sold matches and bought chopsticks there his
whole life (but why did he chop matches if he needed
chopsticks and why they didn't cut up their chopsticks
if they needed matches, I didn't dare to ask).

Happily, I could see him coming a mile off and I
told him I couldn't go away before I'd finished knitting
my jumper. Of course I have my pride so I didn't want
to tell him that I was knitting a jumper for my ex-
husband who fired me – that's the word – after 50 years
of marriage, so I remembered Penelope, Ulysses' wife,

who wove a shroud to buy time. Come to think of it, Penelope was the first navy wife, the first dumb cluck!

It seems that people come back from faraway places like Japan totally transformed, but personally I don't see the value in coming back from holiday totally transformed. I like myself just the way I am and when I look in the mirror I understand even less why your grandfather kicked me out. Well, understand is a big word because I know full well what's inside that brute's battered old head, he's damaged it, more than enough, due to being a boxer. At the moment my mind keeps going back to a Normandy beach which Napoleon and I reached early one morning, far greater a journey than travelling to Japan, I'm sure he's forgotten it, he isn't the sentimental type, but I remember for both of us.

Definitely don't go and tell him that I'm confiding these things to you. He'll think I'm hung up on him, whereas I'm going to let the old fool marinate in his loneliness and too bad for him, he's the one who'll go down on his knees to have me back. Anyway, Ed (Edouard) asked me when the jumper would be finished so he could take care of the plane tickets and I told him I was only on the sleeves so we could take our time. Actually I'm halfway through the body, I knit faster than my shadow, he seems a bit angry and suspicious of the situation, well, just then he pressed down with both hands as he was about to pounce on me and kiss me, as if he was still 20, but the problem is that he put his right hand on the Korean barbecue grill built into the table. That stopped him in his tracks and he let out a scream, leaping off the floor with the grill stuck to his hand, it went hiss-s-s, and you can bet your life his desire to kiss me was gone.

We had to call an ambulance and as we waited he clenched his jaw to keep up appearances but he was suffering like a dog as the grill continued to roast his hand. It smelled like a hog roast but I didn't tell him that, he kept calm by reciting a couple of haikus, a type of Japanese poem.

They had to put a big bandage on his fist and the tears welled up in my eyes because it made me think of your grandfather. I was cross with myself for thinking of that old brute when it was my fault that Ed was suffering before my eyes. The medics put him in the ambulance but not before he made me promise that we'd take the first flight to Japan as soon as he'd recovered, and I did promise because he was in a state where he required a bit of moral support and he left me with a lovely smile and said through gritted teeth, 'Love hurts.'

The ambulance doors closed and I had to go home alone, thinking of your brute of a grandfather and of Ed's words. There was a lot of truth in them, those words. Your grandfather must have looked magnificent in his white robe, it's a pity I never got to see him fight, and you'll laugh at this, I asked him to get dressed up in his boxing kit just for me. It's a real shame that he stopped after that match against Rocky. I encouraged him to go back into the ring, but it was no use, he wouldn't hear a word of it, he must have told you that the match was rigged, and that's sort of true. After the ambulance left, I sat down on a bench, a kind of moist cooling breeze was coming off the lake, subtle and delicate. I was both heavy- and light-hearted at the same time without knowing if it was joy at my past life or sadness about the present. I'll always see him with the eyes of the young traveller I was back then and I feel as if there are still a few grains of sand stuck between my toes. Look after him because he's the kind of man who wouldn't have a clue how to get by on his own, dancing into his old age without realising that the referee is about to ring the final bell.

In other news, your mother told me you're coming for Christmas. Can you write down the names of your grandfather's boxing gloves and bowling ball on a piece of paper for me because I'm really not sure of the spelling. I think it's in English or American, but don't make any mistakes while copying it because it would be annoying to have to unpick the whole thing because of a simple spelling error.

Your loving grandma

PS. When you visit I'll tell you about haikus, you'll see they're very relaxing

PPS. As you've noticed I'm getting better with my punctuation, can you tell?

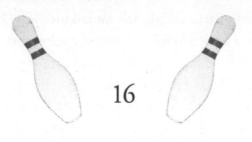

16

My father was largely counting on the element of surprise.

'We won't warn him, then, but at the very last moment, we'll go and pick him up. He won't be able to refuse. When he gets here we'll hit him with lobster, salt pork with lentils and carrots (his favourite dish), cake, candles, "Happy Birthday", childhood memories and the rest of it. We'll pull out all the stops! We'll tug at his heartstrings, you'll see!'

He gazed at the tips of his shoes and added, 'Hold on, I'll even change out of these square-toed shoes he hates so much. I'll go the whole hog.'

At the last minute, just as he was getting ready to drive over and pick up Napoleon, he had a flash of inspiration. 'Hey, why don't you go and get him?' he asked me.

'Me?'

'Yes, it'd be good. You arrive, all relaxed, and say nonchalantly, "Come over for dinner." Just like that, play it cool.
He won't suspect anything if it's you. Got that?'

'Yeah, I've got it. Very Machiavellian, Dad.'

'You don't breathe a word about our plan, obviously. You
just say we wanted to see him.' Here, he drew himself up on
his tiptoes, laid a hand on my shoulder and declared, 'You'll
be my undercover agent.'

Before I could even knock on his door Napoleon called,
'Come in, pal.'

I went in.

It was like a mirage: there he was in the middle of the
living room, dressed up like a lord. The most incredible thing,
however, was that he was standing ramrod straight, his hand
resting nonchalantly on the arm of his wheelchair, his legs
crossed, cloaked in a regal aura that complemented his white
suit and his hair. He looked dazzling.

'You're standing, Grandpa! You can stand on your own
two feet!'

'As you can see, pal. I told you: only a bit of backache.
Call him a doctor? You're having a laugh! Think you can
fool a boxer like that?'

He smiled, looking casual and relaxed with his handsome
head of white hair, which he had slicked back painstakingly
with Brylcreem. A cloud of eau de cologne rose from him.
My emperor was in supreme condition.

Soon, however, I noticed that the arm with which he was supporting himself on the wheelchair was shaking ever so slightly. His smile contained a hint of a grimace, and his forehead glittered with tiny translucent beads.

I had a wonderful portrait of my grandfather before me, and I didn't want to see it ripped apart before my eyes.

'Sit down,' I said. 'I've got something to tell you.'

He didn't need asking twice. 'Right you are. Chiefs of staff always sit while conferring.' He mopped his brow and declared, 'I'm listening.'

He did indeed listen to me with the utmost attention before exploding with laughter. 'That's the best he could come up with? We're out of here, pal. Let's have some fun.'

He put on his faithful black jacket with the ripped pockets that clashed with his white outfit. He hesitated.

'Hang on a sec. I've been meaning to do this for a very long time, but this evening is my opportunity. You're no longer my aide-de-camp.'

'Really?'

'From this evening on, you're my major general – the general with whom I shall fight my final battles!'

I helped him in behind the wheel of the Peugeot 404. It was a cold but clear night. The starry vault curved overhead.

'How about we just drive, pal? Just drive without stopping. Well, only to eat a sandwich at a service station or sleep in a car park somewhere.'

'OK, Grandpa. That'd be great. Where should we go?'

'Just drive. That way. To the sea. To adventure and freedom. Drive until—'

He stopped at a red light, and although it soon turned green, he stayed put.

'You see, pal, it's odd. Sometimes I get the feeling that I remember everything, and at others it's like steam evaporating. Even Rocky. Sometimes I have to think for about ten minutes until I recognise him. I say to myself: "Hmm, this guy reminds me of someone."'

My heart tightened. All the things we would never do again together, and all the events in my life that he would never experience, threatened to choke me.

A car behind us beeped its horn.

'Everyone's always in such a rush!' Napoleon cried. 'Well, I suppose we could at least go and get some good food.'

Napoleon had a huge pile of pink shells on his plate. Crabs, lobsters, langoustines: my father was testing the old adage that the way to a man's heart was through his stomach. My grandfather had shattered the crustaceans without using a cracker, only his fists.

My mother served the salt pork with lentils, the simple yet invigorating dish that my grandfather loved.

'You're having a whale of a time, aren't you?' my father asked.

'Rather salt pork than a motorway sandwich!'

My parents exchanged bemused glances as Napoleon cackled loudly and began to shovel the lentils into his mouth, only looking up to say, 'Gives you gas, but what the hell.'

This final elegant flourish torpedoed the conversation for a while. In any case, we made such an effort to avoid the many topics that might send the situation into meltdown that silence was the only option.

'The weather's freezing at the moment!' my father finally blurted out.

'Yeah,' Napoleon replied. 'It isn't warm. Especially in your house. No problem back home. Must be something to do with the atmosphere here.'

My father pretended he hadn't heard and started to stack the dirty plates.

'Are you changing the plates?' asked Napoleon.

'For cheese.'

'No need. I brought my Opinel with me,' my grandfather said. He patted the pocket where he kept the famous penknife he always whipped out at some point during a meal.

'Ta-da! We're really going to town today in your honour. It isn't your birthday every day. What the heck – we're celebrating!'

Napoleon crossed his arms as he listened to his son.

'You're actually quite a nice son,' he said, his tone neutral.

My father's face cracked into a grateful smile, and he tried to catch my mother's eye to share his joy, which was too great to be contained.

'Not very smart, but quite nice,' Napoleon continued. 'Josephine was right.'

'What's Josephine got to do with this?' my father asked in a toneless voice. 'What do you mean?'

'Nothing special.'

'Whatever. You must admit it's great that we're all here this evening. It's nice to have a get-together, isn't it?'

My mother had left the table but now she returned with a cheeseboard that Napoleon examined carefully.

'Wow, what a platter! Thanks, Sammy!' Napoleon said to my dad.

I was touched to see the surprise on my father's face as he said, 'It's been such a long time since you called me by my first name. It makes me happy. I'd begun to think you'd forgotten it.'

'Actually, I had. I had to look it up on your birth certificate this morning.'

Napoleon hid a gloating half-smile before sniffing the cheese and solemnly declaring, 'They stink just as they ought to. I thought you only liked supermarket cheese.'

He took out his penknife, and its shiny blade glinted as he held it up. He ran the pad of his thumb over it to check that it was sharp.

'I know how much you love cheese,' my father said. 'I remember always choosing Camembert at the school canteen when I was young. To be like you.'

'Stop it, you'll set me blubbing.'

'Oh, come on. Admit you're emotional. You're surprised I remember all of this, aren't you?'

Napoleon sniggered. 'Oh, it's not really that which surprises me . . . '

My father's chin was quivering. For a few seconds I thought Napoleon was trying to make my dad burst into tears and that only my mother's presence was keeping his sobbing at bay.

'And . . . what is it that surprises you, Dad?' he finally managed to say.

'You really want to know? What surprises me, you know, is all this fuss . . . What's this all about, eh? Lobsters . . . salt pork, silly little childhood reminiscences . . . It must be important if you've even taken off your square-toed shoes!'

He cut off a piece of Camembert, stabbed it with his penknife, raised it to eye level and studied it as if it were a gold nugget. He bit into it and chewed noisily, looking sadly at my father all the while.

'You're asking why we invited you?' my father whispered. 'Because it's your birthday, Dad! To see you and spend some time with you. That's all. But nothing's ever simple with you, is it? Also, as we're going to be at Josephine's for Christmas, we thought that . . . We're family, after all. We even got you a cake.'

'Oh, how touching!' said Napoleon, pretending to wipe

a tear from his cheek. 'And apart from drowning me in whipped cream, what's the big idea?'

At this my mother walked over to my grandfather and stroked his head in a gesture that was so graceful and so intimate that time seemed to stand still for a few seconds.

'Napoleon,' she whispered. 'You're exaggerating things, believe me. You don't realise how heartfelt your son's intentions are . . .'

My grandfather shrugged. 'Oh, so he has a heart, has he? That's good to hear.'

'Most certainly. A big, big heart, in fact.'

'If you say so. You'd need to cut him open to find it, mind you.' He stared my father straight in the eye and added, 'Come on then, out with it!'

My father took a deep breath. 'We wanted to tell you that you cannot go on living on your own.'

'Aha, now we're getting to the nitty-gritty. I was starting to think that it would never come out. I can't go on living alone, no less. The scoop of the century! Have you told the newspapers?'

Napoleon drew an old sharpened match from his breast pocket and inserted it between two of his teeth. It got stuck and poked out horizontally.

'Yes, Dad. We've got to face the facts: the divorce, starting over, your fall, the way you acted towards Irene. And, to top it all, last week . . . Can you tell me what on earth you were doing in Chartres in the middle of the night?'

'That's your version of events. I don't remember a thing. Except for your face at dawn and your square toes. An unforgettable wake-up call.'

'Exactly. That's what makes it all the more worrying. There's a very good home opposite the school. They'll spoil you there. What do you say?'

'I say this Cammie's a beauty. I recall finding a fantastic Camembert in Boston in 1952. In Boston. In 1952. Imagine that!' He started sniffing the tip of his toothpick.

'Stop it. That's disgusting!' cried my father.

'Less disgusting than what you're suggesting!'

He shut one eye in order to take aim at the bin and launched his toothpick, but it landed in a flowerpot.

'Missed!' he said with a provocative grin.

'We thought,' my father continued, 'you might one day feel like having some friends and doing all kinds of activities. Apparently they do pottery there, you know.'

'Oh, for Christ's sake, pottery . . .'

'Anyway, there will be people to take care of you. Are you really not tempted by the idea of being with other people like yourself?'

'Can you tell me what you mean by "like yourself"?' asked Napoleon in an icy tone.

My father loosened his shirt collar.

Napoleon tried again. 'Put simply: you want to deport me. Right?'

'You're talking gibberish now, Dad. We're not talking

about a concentration camp but a welcome home.'

'Welcome my arse, eh pal!' Napoleon whispered to me.

I smiled, and my father asked me quietly, 'What did he say?'

'Oh, nothing. Just that you're extremely kind.'

My father took several steps towards Napoleon and crouched down so that they were at the same height.

'You know, Dad . . . a home where they'll look after you, where you won't put yourself in danger and where you'll have fun. He sighed and said, gently, 'Face the facts: all your mates are gone.'

'They were weak, that's all. Didn't do enough sport.'

'We'll come and visit you often. It's just around the corner. It's a really nice place with a swimming pool and the gardens are filled with forsythias.'

'Forsythia smells of piss,' declared Napoleon.

'I honestly don't see any similarity between a home that costs me an arm and a leg and a concentration camp.'

'However luxurious, no one goes in there of their own free will, and no one comes out alive – those are two things they have in common!'

My father gave another disheartened sigh. He patted Napoleon's knee and stood up. 'Well, if you'd prefer to live alone in a house that's as ancient as you are until you set fire to it, or lock yourself in the boot of your 404, then be my guest.'

'You said it, you chump, and I do feel free. Have our

negotiations broken down?' asked Napoleon with a smile.

My father put on his best cheerful voice. 'OK, time out. Let's cut your cake. Just the kind you like, with lots of whipped cream. That'll cheer us all up.'

'Too true!' said Napoleon.

My mother brought in the cake very slowly so that the candles didn't go out.

'Take a deep breath, Dad. We'll give you a hand if you don't manage to blow them all out.'

One ... two ... and ... Seconds later, my father's face was spattered with whipped cream projected by the stream of air from Napoleon's mouth.

'What did you say?' Napoleon enquired. 'You wanted to help me?' Giving my mother a cheeky look, he added, 'That was good. The cream, I mean.'

My father looked like a clown, and I could see that Napoleon's game, his dance around my father, had gone too far. My father was angry and humiliated, his arms hanging loosely by his sides. I had to look down at the floor.

'You know what your problem is, Dad?' he suddenly said, his voice trembling. 'Well, you're going to find out.' And with that he disappeared.

'Where's he off to?' asked Napoleon with a puzzled look at my mother. 'What's got into him? We were having a good laugh and then—'

'No, Napoleon, we weren't having a laugh. You're hurting me too.' My mother was shaking.

'Forgive me. Collateral damage.'

'Your son doesn't deserve this treatment.'

'He can go to his old idiots' home himself if he thinks it's so great.'

The basement door slammed shut, and a few seconds later my father appeared.

'Is this what you want?' he shouted in a completely unfamiliar voice. 'Is this how you'd like me to be? *Would* have liked me to be, *Dad*. That word annoys you, eh? *Dad, Dad, Dad.*'

He was holding up two large boxing gloves.

Surprised and caught off guard, Napoleon tried to crack a joke, but no sound came out of his mouth. All he could do was grumble, 'Stop it.'

My father made clumsy circular motions with his fists in front of his chest, like a marionette. Sensing that he was scoring a few points, he started to skip about.

'Stop your silly act, damn it!' said Napoleon.

But my father pounced on this apparent breach in Napoleon's defences. He threw several weak punches, hopped gracelessly from one foot to the other and got into position behind a woefully inadequate guard. His belly wobbled a bit as he moved. He was a terrible, ridiculous caricature of a boxer, but I could see he was delighted to have gained the upper hand.

'Is this how you wanted me to be, huh? Would it have made me your true son? These bloody boxing gloves were the only possible route to your affections.'

'Stop, stop,' said Napoleon.

He covered his eyes with his arms as if the punches my father was aiming at thin air were jabs landing on him. I'd never seen Napoleon on the defensive like this.

'Yes. Maybe in the ring you'd have taken me a bit more seriously. Maybe in your eyes I'd have been something other than a clown. The thing is, though – we don't get to choose. I'm not like you. You should get that into that battered old skull of yours!'

'Sod this, I'm leaving,' said Napoleon. 'I'm getting out of this damn house!'

'Where are you going?' cried my father.

'I'm out of here. I think I've stored a grenade somewhere in the basement. I'm going to show your old folks one hell of a party. Let me through.'

He tried to manoeuvre his wheelchair to leave the house – to retreat – but my father was blocking his path.

In the space of a second – what am I talking about? Not a second, a flash – we saw my father strike a real boxer's pose. On his guard, his weight on his front foot, his shoulders rounded, alert behind his gloves, his knees solid and supple – the instinctive posture of a great boxer.

This spectacle, which lasted no longer than a single heartbeat, struck my emperor and me like a bolt from the blue. This vision seemed to scorch Napoleon, and he was very close to breaking down in tears.

But then it was all over. Shocked and stunned by his own

audacity, my father stared at his gloves as if astonished to find them there.

'See?' my father said. 'You didn't even deem me worthy of a new pair. They were always too big for me. And they stink. Where did you pick them up?'

My mother signalled to my father to tone it down a bit. Napoleon had lost the battle, and there was no point in rubbing his face in it any longer. He turned his back on us to face the French windows through which he watched a light sleet falling from the dark sky.

Suddenly Napoleon spun round and declared, 'Now that you've finished messing about, you know what I'd really like?'

17

Saturday night at Melun bowling alley. Full of young people and buckets of alcohol. Some were there to forget that they did not have a job to go to on Monday – and the rest that they did. A single obsession was reflected in all their eyes: a ball and ten pins.

Napoleon high-fived some people and bumped fists with others. His favourite lane had been reserved for him. He led my parents to the shoe hire counter.

'Size seven and eleven?' the assistant said. 'No problem for the lady, but for the gentleman all I have left is a pair of size nines ...'

'That's fine,' said Napoleon. 'It's absolutely fine. It's always good to get them a little on the small side.'

While my parents put on theirs, I helped my grandfather slip his feet into his own special bowling shoes.

'Don't forget the double knot, pal.' He immediately began to limber up by revolving his arms.

'It looks easy,' my father said as he watched other players taking their run-ups. 'The shoes, though – I don't know but I feel as if . . . ' He was having trouble walking. His toes were curled inwards and he was leaning on my mother's shoulder.

'Are you sure they're not too small?' she asked my grandfather. 'He's in a lot of pain, you know.'

'I told you that you should always get them a little small,' Napoleon said. 'Of course, if you will insist on wearing ones with square toes . . . Come on – let's get going. Do you need the bumpers up to help you?'

'No way. You'll see.'

We did see. Two hours later, my father still hadn't knocked over a single pin and had dropped his ball on his toe five times and banged himself on the nose with it. My father limped during his run-up and his ball seemed glued to his hand when he tried to release it. It bounced lamely on the wooden floor a few times and invariably ended up in the gutter.

Meanwhile, Napoleon launched his ball gracefully and casually from his wheelchair, which I pushed across the boards. He turned his back on the lane before the ball had even reached the pins and shouted 'Strike!' when he heard them cannon together. Occasionally he would make a mess of his throw and, purely from the sound of the pins falling, he was able to conclude, 'Oh, one of those little ladies is acting up! The one in the middle.'

My mother had soon given up, but she appeared to enjoy watching the games.

'Now, concentrate this time!' Napoleon urged my father. 'One last shot. One final flourish. Relax – you're all tense.'

'Nice joke,' my father grumbled. 'You should try bowling straight in these shoes.'

'I told you that they need to be on the small side. Come on – let one rip and you'll feel a whole lot better.'

This classy comment triggered uproarious laughter around us.

'Leave me alone, will you.'

My grandfather winked at me and whispered, 'The greatest battles are won at the last minute. Remember that, pal.' I would later recall those words with a mixture of affection and grief.

'What did he say?' my father asked, as he was about to begin his run-up.

'Oh, nothing. Only that you've taken up the correct position.'

He launched into his approach, but instead of leaving his hand, the ball remained wedged onto his fingers and dragged my father forward, flat on his tummy and head first, towards the pins.

'What an effing strike!' my grandfather mumbled. 'It may be controversial stylistically, but full marks for creativity.'

Having extracted his head from the pile of skittles, my father staggered back towards us, with several scrapes on his chin and his fingers still pinned inside the ball, through a row of players who greeted him with a mixture of cheers and jibes. He took refuge by my mother's side, and she attempted to remove the ball.

'It's no use,' she said. 'It won't come off. Your fingers must have swollen.'

'Quite honestly, darling, I've had enough. Remind me to forget his birthday next year.'

My mother stopped and stared, then she took a step backwards and studied my father very closely.

'What is it?' my father asked. 'Why are you looking at me like that?'

'No particular reason. I just find you amazingly handsome.'

'With this ball, my bashed-in face and my pigeon toes?'

'Very handsome, because you're very fragile. All that is fragile is beautiful, don't you think?'

My father shrugged and held up his ball. 'I promise to think about that, but for the moment I have more pressing concerns.'

He turned to Napoleon and said, 'You planned this whole thing, didn't you? Even this was a set-up, right?'

Napoleon merely shrugged and lifted his black ball with one hand. 'I choose to ignore that. Right, my go.'

A look, a slight wiggle of his forefinger and I

understood that I was to let my emperor take centre stage. On his own.

All of a sudden, as if catapulted from his chair by an ejector device, he stood up. My father's jaw nearly hit the floor and he slumped onto the seat beside my mother.

There was total silence. Not a pin fell, not a single ball rolled. The chorus of players gathered around all chanted in unison, 'Ohhhhhhhh!'

Napoleon was a little unsteady, his steps shuffling and mechanical, but he advanced imperiously towards the lane, sweeping the audience with a proud and dominant gaze. The emperor in all his immortal majesty.

Three more yards, two, one ... He was standing at the top of his lane.

A short run-up, a few strides, and he eased himself into a position so that he was almost doing the splits. Right leg back, left leg thrust forward at a right angle, knees locked. Perfect, artistic geometry. His ball flew from his hand with the grace of a blackbird regaining its freedom.

Everyone rubbed their eyes. Suddenly two hands clapped, then four, then ten and soon the applause swelled to a thunderous torrent. Napoleon bowed to his admirers.

I alone saw his smile harden, his jaw tighten and his frame sway imperceptibly. Like the trees in my dream. I discreetly moved his wheelchair closer. He sat down elegantly, a smile on his lips. Perfect timing – he was exhausted.

'Thanks, pal. Another ten seconds and I'd have collapsed!

They'd have deported me in the blink of an eye.' He said this to me out of earshot of anyone else.

'What did he say?' my father asked.

'Oh, nothing. Only that he'd love to go dancing now!'

An hour later I said goodbye to him at his home. It was snowing, and his wheelchair slithered on the ground. We weren't going to see each other for several days. The holidays were about to start, and we'd soon be leaving to stay with Josephine.

'Do you want me to give her a message?'

'Tell her everything's OK, pal.'

Snowflakes began to settle on the windowpane.

'And that I think of her,' he added. 'A bit. Not every day, but a bit.' He thought for a couple of seconds before adding, 'Oh, damn it – tell her I think of her often.'

I helped him to his bed. His bedclothes seemed to swamp his body. He beckoned to me and whispered into my ear, 'My pal, lots of things slip my mind at the moment. Most of them I couldn't care less about, but there is the name of that beach ... I've spent entire nights trying to find it, but it's no use. You know, Josephine's beach. So if you could ...'

'I promise I will. Don't lose any more sleep over it.'

18

Two days later we dropped Endov at Napoleon's house and set off by car for Josephine's place in the south through a relentless curtain of rain.

My father hadn't mentioned Napoleon's stunt since the birthday meal and the bowling outing. Our conversations had either revolved entirely around his bank and the responsibilities it imposed on him, or around my school results, which he considered impeccable.

We needed to stop to fill up the car. My father was so lost in his daydreams that he let the petrol overflow the tank. Later, he stopped too far from the machine at the toll booth to be able to slide in his card and so he had to squeeze through the gap between the car door and the concrete island to get close enough to pay. Having finally completed this operation, he sat staring straight ahead for an eternity after the barrier had been raised.

Then, very solemnly, as if the words had been waiting to come out for days, he said, 'I've had an idea. You'll probably find it odd, but here we go ... What if he were ... um ...'

'If he were what?' my mother asked.

'I don't know. The other day he stood on his own two feet. Clear as daylight. We all saw it. I didn't dream it, did I?'

'No.'

'And yet, if you recall, the doctor said he'd never be able to stand again. Move his legs, yes; get to his feet, no. Remember how explicit he was? What if he had, I don't know, some substance that regenerated him. A sort of serum. I've read about them at the library. Apparently there are some insects that can live for a hundred and twenty, even a hundred and fifty years.'

'Oh, come on,' said my mother. 'Your father isn't an insect.' Seeing that this answer wasn't to her husband's liking, she added, 'It is true, though. It's strange how he confounds science.'

'I also remember,' my father said, 'how we used to go on holiday not far from a nuclear power station when I was small. We swam in water that was very warm and slightly green. He told us it was from aquifers, but maybe ... There was seaweed everywhere, and Napoleon said that it was good for your health and tasted nice in salad. A bit of random radiation and bang! You turn into ...' Although he was driving, he turned to look at me in the back seat. 'Maybe Napoleon's a mutant, Leonard!'

*

Josephine showed me her knitting that same evening. The sleeves were finished, as was half of the body. Now the most difficult job was to work the words 'Born to Win' into the white wool.

'It'll be ready in a few weeks' time,' she sighed. 'You know my suitor, Edouard ... That's all he's waiting for before he whisks me off to Asia.' A mischievous smile playing on her lips, she went on, 'It's funny – I didn't think I could still be kidnapped. You don't feel like giving that piece of wool a tug, do you?'

'It'll unravel the whole jumper,' I said uncertainly.

'Precisely. Go on, just a couple of rows. To buy some time. It's a classic ruse – people have been doing it for centuries.' But then, realising the amount of wool that was winding into a heap, her tone grew more sombre. 'Not too much, though. I want Napoleon to have time to wear it for a while, you see. That's the trouble with time: you never know if you need to waste it or buy it!'

The very next morning I showed her Alexandre's cap. She examined it and promised to mend it. I pointed out the small label sewn onto the side of the hat.

'You must leave the two initials there. RR. R for Rawcziik, with two "I"s. I don't know what the other R stands for. I think those two initials mean a lot to him.'

Josephine was well. She'd even put on a little weight, and her fuller face made her look younger, but there was a constant but discreet aura of sadness that she wore close to her chest like a locket. She struck me as being much younger than Napoleon, and it was almost hard to picture them together.

What was he up to right now? I couldn't help picturing him alone in his bed, his arms and clenched fists stretched out alongside his tiny body. I also tried to imagine what Christmas might be like for Alexandre Rawcziik, but I couldn't.

My mother wasted no time in unpacking her drawing materials. She spent most of her days sitting on a stone bench in the garden with her sketchbook on her knees, lost in her own world of paper and pastels.

For his part my father had decided to tidy the old barn. I went shopping with Josephine to carry the bags. She greeted everyone and asked after this person and that as if she'd lived here all her life. I watched her fill out her tricast betting slips over a cup of coffee.

'I haven't the foggiest idea about the runners. I select them at random.'

We checked her results the next day. Her horses always came in last.

I shelled kilos and kilos of beans, but we never cooked them.

'The only thing I like about beans,' she revealed to me, 'is shelling them! It keeps me calm. My mind is empty while I'm doing it. It's my equivalent of bowling!'

Otherwise, she and I watched mindless crime series that

gave away the culprit's identity within the first five minutes, while she mended Alexandre's cap.

In fact, we all wanted to talk about the elephant in the room: Napoleon. His absence echoed in the gaps in our conversations, his face and his thick white hair floated over the weeds in the garden and his clenched fists banged on the frosted windowpanes.

'You know,' Josephine said to me a few days after our arrival, 'I wonder if I might not be better off in an old people's home rather than gallivanting around Asia. You can rest without having to take care of anything. I've always liked old people's homes.' She signalled with a raised finger for me to come closer and whispered, 'Don't repeat this, but a few months ago, just before our divorce, I enquired about double rooms. I never dared mention it to your brute of a grandfather, though.'

I wondered how my lovely grandmother had been able to live with the tornado that was Napoleon, and I told myself that one's permanent rebellion depends on another's gentle resignation.

One evening as we were busy sorting lentils, my thoughts strayed to the picture of Rocky and I asked my grandmother, 'Do you remember Rocky?'

I saw her fingers freeze among the lentils. 'Rocky? Wait a second . . .'

'Napoleon's final opponent.'

'OK, now I'm with you. The Italian in that rigged match!'

The rigged match. That old refrain. The rigged match.

'What made you think of that?' Josephine asked. 'It's so long ago. It doesn't matter any more. The whole world's forgotten about Napoleon and Rocky. Rocky's been dead for decades and Napoleon's—' She fell silent for a while before going on. 'A boxer's reign is short and disappointing.'

I caught my breath. 'There's one thing I don't understand. Rocky died a few weeks after that last fight. He must have been tired against Napoleon.'

Josephine stared straight ahead. I wondered whether she had heard me. I continued, 'So how come Napoleon didn't knock him out? He was in great shape at the time. For the first five rounds he threw everything at Rocky and then, all of a sudden, after the break, he had no strength left in his arms, none in his legs either – he was like a puppet. A powder puff. I found an old newspaper clipping about it. Rocky gets the upper hand again and wins on points.'

Josephine looked right at me. I was struck, and even a little scared, by her eyes. They were like darts. 'I have something to share with you,' she said.

My pulse started to race. 'About Ro-Rocky?' I stammered.

Josephine shrugged. 'No ... Something Edouard introduced me to. Something amazing.' Narrowing her eyes, raising one finger until it was level with her nose and adopting a voice of great wisdom, she slowly recited, '*Listen to the grass; the wind. A passing lark.*'

Several seconds of silence, then she spoke again. '*Come the time, watch the silence. Eye intrudes.*'

Her head was rocking as if it were swaying in a gentle breeze, as if she were deep in the heart of time.

'What are those, Grandma? Grass, wind and an eye watching silence?'

'Haikus.'

'Haikos?'

'Ku. Hai-kus. Japanese poems.'

They were short, beautiful and strange. As limpid as my mother's drawings. Josephine had learned all about them from Edouard.

'A haiku tries to capture the evanescence of things, you see?'

'I don't know what "evanescence" means.'

'Evanescence is when a thing is on the point of vanishing and you have to catch it before it disappears for ever. That's basically it: a haiku is a way of capturing the final moment of something.'

I reckoned that it was her age that allowed her to under-stand the philosophy of evanescence.

'Want to hear another? Hold on . . . *A smudge of shadow. Clouds in the sky before a three-master.* Now you have a go.'

'Should I?'

'Of course. All you need to do is concentrate very hard on a living thing or a display of nature and then try to merge with that thing or scene. And once you're there, try to imagine the seconds just before it disappears.'

I might as well have a go. I started by thinking of my mother and her drawings, but then the large trees of my dreams bubbled up into my mind. I imagined bark covering my skin.

'*Large trees lying like men. Roots in mid-air; hair in the sky.*'

'Brilliant! You're a dab hand at haikus. That's great.'

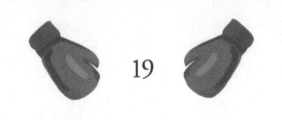

19

We celebrated Christmas as best we could, but in lacklustre fashion, almost in slow motion.

We chose our words carefully, steering clear of fragile memories. The presents were a distraction: Josephine gave me a remote-controlled motorbike which briefly put a wild and carefree spring in my step. My father had bought her a large-screen television, which he went out to fetch from the boot of our car.

'That's kind of you, but I already have one.'

'It doesn't matter,' my father replied. 'This one's even better. It has an ultra-flat screen and a high-definition display. And, what's more, it has a remote control!'

She thanked him, although she still preferred her old one. She did, however, announce that she would never use the remote.

'Why not?' my father asked.

'That's just how it is. It would mean I'd surrendered. Napoleon categorically refused to take the lift in the metro and would take the stairs instead. He said it would spell the beginning of the end. Well, I'm the same. Starting to use a remote control would mean I'd grown old – I can still get up to change the channel myself, you know!'

I helped my father to set up the flat-screen. He didn't have a clue about plugs and things. The huge set lit up. We all expected to see Napoleon appear on the screen. But no, it was a programme about camels.

We ate a four-tier cake. Three tiers too many. We felt sluggish and miserable enough as it was.

'Come on,' my father said. 'Let's crack open some champagne. It is Christmas, after all.'

He reminded me of a clown desperately performing tricks to rows of empty seats. Josephine took a sip, hesitantly at first and then with enthusiasm. Within minutes she had emptied her champagne flute, and she demanded a refill that my father didn't dare refuse her. She drained it in one this time before putting on Alexandre's cap, which she'd finished mending. She wiped her lips on her sleeve and let out a little burp, much to her own surprise, as if it were the first one she had ever emitted.

It was then – right then – that everything started to go pear-shaped.

First she went bright red. Next, the fizzing bubbles made

her eyes water. Her jaw clenched so hard that we could see the muscles straining under her skin. And finally she yelled, 'Shit! Damn! Fuck! Bloody hell!'

My parents jumped and I jumped.

Josephine turned to me in one movement. 'I mean, can you tell me what this is really about, all this nonsense about a fresh start. I'll give you a fresh start!'

She must have kept all her emotions bottled up over the course of the evening and since the divorce, and now the champagne bubbles were bringing them all back to the surface again. She was beginning to totter on her feet. My father rushed over.

'Mum, maybe it'd be best if you went to b—'

'Hands off, little Samuel Sunshine. I can stand up straight. A fresh start . . . In spite of his pompous act, I know what's given him the willies. Does he take me for a complete idiot? Think I don't have eyes in my head? He doesn't want me to see him enter his final round, the silly fool.'

'Mum, you're not yourself.'

'I've never been *more* myself! I had to let it all out sooner or later.'

She grabbed a half-empty champagne flute from father's hand and, before he could react, raised it to her lips and knocked back the contents. She let go of the glass, which smashed on the floor.

'Oh, wow!' she exclaimed, stifling a hiccup before bursting out laughing. Then she continued, 'Ahhh, that feels good! All of a sudden I feel full of energy! My word ... All so I don't see him entering his final round! Whereas that's exactly what I wanted – to fight our final battle together. He's such a stubborn old mule that I wouldn't put it past him to leave without ever giving any explanations. Is it still weighing on his mind?'

'Explanations about what?' asked my father, visibly intrigued. 'What do you mean "weighing on his mind"?'

Josephine merely crossed her arms on her chest and went into a sulk. 'Nothing. It's my business. I'd love to start a new life, too, by the way. It seems to be all the rage.'

'This evening?' my father ventured. 'How about we watch television instead?'

'No TV this evening. Oh, look what happened to your remote control!' She got up and vanished for a few seconds into the kitchen, from where her voice could be heard. 'I binned it!' She came back and sat down on the sofa, took off Alexandre's cap and handed it to me. I popped it on my head. 'What about you, Leonard? You know what it takes to start a new life? Huh?'

Out of the corner of my eye I saw my mother taking in every detail of the scene.

'If Napoleon were here,' Josephine went on, 'what would he do to make a new start? I'm waiting.'

She was smiling. My gaze alighted on a promotional leaflet she had received in the post. I pointed to it.

'The Space Shot?' asked Josephine. 'Great! Let's go. No problem.'

I could already see her flying through the air at breakneck speed in a glass capsule connected to two rubber bands from which she would then swing for several minutes.

'Oh no, M-M-Mum!' my father stammered. 'You don't know what you're doing.'

'I know precisely what I'm doing and I grew out of having to ask for your permission a long time ago. Feel free to stay here and watch television.'

The telephone rang shrilly and the same thought shot through all our minds at once. We were all in the room together, and Josephine wasn't expecting any calls on Christmas Day, so we knew it would be Napoleon, sticking his oar in and claiming his seat in the space capsule.

'Perfect timing from the brute,' said Josephine. 'I'm going to give him a piece of my mind!'

She picked up the phone. Her eyes sank to the floor. All she said, in a slightly disappointed tone of voice, was, 'Oh, it's you. I sound strange? No, no, not in the least. Yes, yes, that's right – Happy Christmas to you too. Oh, yes, and Happy Easter while we're at it. No, I'm not acting weirdly.' She covered the mouthpiece with her hand and whispered, 'It's Edouard.'

She listened for several minutes to what Edouard was saying, her eyes glazing over slightly. She suddenly froze.

'Get married? To you? Well, actually . . . why not? You're in luck – I'm in full fresh-start mode. Am I tipsy? By golly, no – I'm perfectly in control. I'll think about it. Yes, all right,

I'll give you an answer very soon.' She hung up with a cackle. 'He had it coming. "Born to Win", indeed! He thinks I'm going to wait for him until the cows come home? Now, let's board that space capsule.'

While she was looking in her room for something to keep her warm, my slightly dazed-looking father said to my mother, 'Tell me if I've missed something, but just now my mother . . .'

'Yes?'

'She just accepted a marriage proposal?'

My mother pursed her lips. 'It sounded like it.'

The fairground was jam-packed with people, and a dazzling halo of light rose into the night sky like a circle of blue fire. Josephine was staggering a little, and we had to support her occasionally. The Space Shot ride dominated the fair as if throwing down the gauntlet to visitors, lighting people's faces with expressions of terror.

'There it is,' said Josephine. 'I'll be a different person when I step out of that thing. And it'll be the start of a new life for me, too.'

'Are you sure, Mum? Because, you know, sometimes we do things and then the next day . . . Hey, how about the dodgems over there? They give you a good shake, too.'

'Tut tut, don't talk to me as if I'm demented, and keep your philosophising to yourself. Just because I wasn't a boxer like Napoleon doesn't mean I'm not entitled to my own fresh start.'

She was silent for a few moments and then said, 'Eternity's for sharing!' She was swaying from the alcohol.

We must have lied about our ages when we got to the ride, because I was a little under the minimum height. Grandma was over another kind of limit, but they let us through anyway.

Three minutes later we were inside the capsule with our feet dangling in the air. I was scared witless, and Josephine couldn't stop giggling. In a few seconds the rubber bands would be fully stretched. My parents were watching us with horror.

An onlooker remarked of Josephine, 'She's got some guts!'

'That's my mother!' my father proudly proclaimed.

The countdown started. Time for last requests.

'Grandma?'

'Yes?'

'You know that beach . . .'

'Beach? What beach?'

'You know! Napoleon's beach.'

'Oh yes, Napoleon's beach.'

'If we survive, will you show me where it is?'

'I'll show you a great deal more than that!'

Josephine threw up three times on the drive home. Each time she wagged her finger, my father pulled over to the side of the road and she leaped out.

'I'm getting a bit fed up with this,' my father grumbled.

'Can't they behave a bit better at their age? I can understand with my father, at least – I was used to it. I've known for as long as I can remember that he's a ticking time bomb and that his favourite pastime is making my life hell. But Josephine! Gentle Josephine … And now this marriage thing. I need a holiday, a real holiday in a place where no one comes along to ruin your life, where they look after you and everyone's at your beck and call.'

'It's called an old people's home!' said my mother.

'What were you ruffians saying?' Josephine asked as she jumped back into the car. Within seconds she'd fallen asleep and was snoring like a freight train. When we got home we carried her, still comatose, to the sofa. The three of us stood there looking at her.

'It's funny how they look so harmless when they're sleeping,' said my father. 'But as soon as they open one eye it's like a bull run!'

Josephine raised an eyebrow as if she'd heard him and then opened one eye.

'Feeling better, Mum?'

'Yes,' she said curtly.

'Shall we go to bed? I think the party's over.'

'Not entirely, it isn't. Pass me the phone. I've done some thinking.'

'Oh, good,' my father said with evident relief. 'I'm happy to see you're being sensible. Night truly is the mother of counsel. Sometimes, after a drink or two, we say things …'

He handed her the phone. She immediately dialled a number.

'Hello. Edouard? Yes, this is Josephine. I accept your proposal. I've completed my jumper. Wherever you want! Asia? Whatever floats your boat. Along the Mekong? Perfect! We can go to Patagonia if you like. It isn't in Asia? Really! Anyway, I'm ready for a new life.'

She hung up and whispered, 'Too bad for Napoleon! Hey-ho, he should never have gone!'

Noting the disapproving look on my father's face, she snapped, 'Got something to say to me?'

My father shook his head slowly. His shell-shocked expression was a picture of disillusionment and resignation.

'No. No comment.'

'Because you've got your thinking face on.'

He stood up. 'Don't think I'm not finding this enjoyable, because I am, but I think I'll go and get some sleep.'

I was left alone with Josephine. She waited until it was completely quiet and then signalled to me to follow her to her bedroom. There, she took a small bottle of perfume from the drawer of her bedside table and unscrewed the top. She waved the bottle under my nose.

'So?'

'It smells nice. Strange.' It was an indefinable fragrance, a little old-fashioned, a once-marvellous scent that had faded.

'It's the scent of good times. Put your hand on top of the bottle.'

She tipped up the little bottle. Sand. Red sand mixed with grains of mica, which still retained their original sparkle.

'Whoops, not too much. I need to keep some for when I grow old.'

'The beach,' I murmured. The beach of freedom with Napoleon. Sunshine Beach.

'Don't tell the old brute. He'll think it's soppy.'

'OK.' It was the perfect time to whisper to her, 'He thinks of you often, you know. Very often. All the time, in fact.'

'And he can't tell me himself? Got rid of his phone, did he?'

'You know how stubborn he is, but how soft his heart is as well.'

'I'll come back when he tells me to come back. But until that happens, look at this.' She unfolded an old road map on the bed. 'There! That's where it was.'

A tiny yellow smudge had been circled in pencil. The map was worn out and the beach was hidden in a fold. How odd to think that it had all begun on that tiny stretch of beach. It looked as if all the roads on the map led to that remote spot.

'You know what?' my grandmother said.

'No.'

'Sometimes I feel as if I still have a few grains of sand trapped between my toes.'

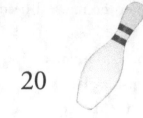

20

The following morning, Mum said the new day should at least be a peaceful one.

'Let's be positive,' she said over breakfast. 'After last night's antics, she's not going to be in any mood for excitement today. We should be able to relax.'

The morning wore on and still Josephine didn't appear.

'Personally,' said my father, 'I'm in no hurry to see her, given all the drama when she's awake. Let's give her some time to recover.'

I tried out my motorbike in the garden but soon grew tired of it and sat down next to my mother to watch her draw. Her gestures were economical and discreet. With a few brushstrokes, the garden, with its trees petrified by winter, seemed to spring from the page.

She let me leaf through her sketchbook. The past few

months flashed before my eyes, and for a few minutes I found myself transported back to the Gare de Lyon in Paris on the day of my grandmother's departure. My mother had even thought to add the clocktower showing the precise time of the separation in the background.

Next, I lingered over the scene of the four of us sitting in the café. There was a gaping hole where Josephine would usually have been.

'Napoleon's pulling a strange face,' I said. 'Are you sure that's how he looked?'

'That's how he looked on the inside.'

I'd never noticed in his expression the hint of melancholy that my mother had highlighted.

'And that's the time Napoleon fell over while dancing to "Barracuda", Mum. You weren't there, though!'

'No. I imagined it. Was that how it looked?'

'Exactly like that. You'd think you were spying on us from somewhere.'

Suddenly I realised that I was actually searching for one specific scene. It was a full-page drawing that jumped out at me.

'I knew that moment made its mark on you,' my mother said. 'Your father looks extremely handsome there, doesn't he?'

Once more, my father's pose took my breath away. I traced the silhouette of my father with my finger, and around his torso, head and raised gloves. I felt a sense of unease.

My mother took back her sketchbook, flicked through it and tore out a page.

'Here, you can give this to your friend.'

It was a sketch of Alexandre Rawcziik's cap. My mother had taken care to emphasise the initials, and I was sure that Alexandre would relish this detail. On paper the cap appeared to be restored to its former glory – it looked brand new.

Just then, my father opened a window and signalled that there was a visitor outside. 'It's the other bloke,' he whispered. 'The suitor.'

Edouard looked like some sort of Father Christmas with his otter-skin hat tied under his chin. His face was round, with a pale complexion but very flushed and with pronounced cheekbones. On his feet he was wearing moonboots, their long tassels trailing on the ground, and under his nose he had a bushy moustache that looked as if it was composed of the same hairs as his boots. I couldn't take my eyes off those shoes.

'Yak hair. I bought them in Outer Mongolia,' he said by way of introduction before bowing ever so slightly and adding, 'I'm Edouard. You may have heard of me.'

I could tell at first glance that he was steeped in traveller's wisdom. He was obviously a featherweight compared with Napoleon, but he had a beaming smile that lent him a friendly air. He held out his right hand, which was still strapped with bandages.

'I burnt myself while tinkering with the engine of my car.'

I was the only person on earth who knew that he was lying, and this lie immediately endeared him to me. He had obviously dropped by to talk to Josephine.

'She isn't awake yet,' my father said in a low voice. 'She had a bit of a . . . heavy night.'

They eventually invited Edouard to take a seat on the sofa, and this was followed by a long silence, since no one could think of anything to say. A while later, as Josephine still hadn't woken up, Edouard opened his satchel.

'Fancy a game?' he asked me, pointing to a long gilded wooden box that looked like an old pen case. A Go set.

He arranged the elements of the game on the coffee table.

'I'll explain something first: the literary name for Go is *ranka*, which means "rotten axe handle".'

'In Chinese?'

He smiled. 'In Japanese. In Chinese it's called *weiki*, meaning "game of encirclement". Anyway, I'll explain why. Legend has it that one day a woodcutter stopped on his route home to watch a game of Go. When he set off again, he noticed that his axe had rusted and that several centuries had passed.'

I nodded to show that I liked the story. There were a few seconds of silence.

'I like explaining things,' he added as if in apology. 'So I explain them.'

He smiled from ear to ear. Dad and Mum looked as

uptight as two people holding their breath so as not to knock down a house of cards.

'Well, you see, this is the *goban*,' Edouard said.

'The what?'

'You really want me to explain?'

'Yes.'

My response made him glow with pleasure.

'So ... the *goban* is the board, if you will. Two intersections are said to be neighbours when they are on the same line without any other intersections between them.'

'OK.'

'Now, I'm going to explain a very important thing: a territory is a set of unoccupied and adjacent intersections, marked by stones of the same colour.'

Next, he talked about live stones, *seki* (mutual life), dead stones and one-eyed stones, about liberties of a chain, chains without liberties and *atari* chains, capture and threats, and compensation points known as *komi*. There were endless exceptions to each of these rules.

It was more complex than bowling, for which you need to know only two words: 'spare' and 'strike'. And, even then, it doesn't really matter if you don't know them because a woman in a bikini sashays across the electronic screen to explain the whole thing.

'You see,' Edouard continued, 'white is not allowed to place a stone on b straight away and take black stone number one, which ...'

I lost interest. All I could see was his moustache waggling before my eyes. His voice blended into one continuous, dreary stream of sound in which I could no longer distinguish the individual words.

'Hey, did you get that explanation?'

I nodded. This appeared to satisfy him.

As Josephine still hadn't appeared, my mother ended up pouring Edouard a cup of tea. Just before he took a sip, he said, 'Those are the basics. I'll explain the advanced rules when I've had my tea. It's very pleasant – and very rare – to meet someone who likes having things explained to him.'

Between sips, Edouard's face grew very earnest as he turned to face my father.

'My dear sir, since Josephine still isn't awake, I shall address my request to you. You see . . .'

'Please,' my father replied, with a smile.

'I have the honour of asking you ... um ... for your mother's hand in marriage.'

Silence settled over the scene. I sensed from the gleam in his eye and the tightening of the skin on his forehead that my father was struggling to get his head around the question.

'Let me explain,' Edouard began again. 'Josephine has agreed to be my wife, but I like to do things in the correct order. Order is the prelude to happiness.'

'If you say so,' my father said.

He scratched his head and exchanged bewildered glances

with my mother. The suitor waited patiently without show-ing any signs of exasperation.

'In Europe,' my father began, 'one usually asks the father, not the son, for a woman's hand in marriage.'

Edouard dismissed this objection with a wave of his hand. 'A trifle. Let me explain something: in the Shinto tradition, the father and the son—'

'No, OK, it's fine. Do whatever you want, but stop explaining things to me. Get married or don't get married: I don't give a d—' Without finishing his sentence, he turned to my mother and said, 'Good God, they drive you mad at this age,' before turning his attention to a book of cross-word puzzles.

'I know you don't want to,' my mother said, as she tried to diffuse the situation, 'but I feel like watching something entertaining on TV. Something simple and fun. A film, something escapist.'

Edouard produced a DVD from his satchel. 'I have exactly what we need,' he said happily. 'I was planning to watch it with Josephine, but it doesn't matter. I know it by heart, anyway. You'll see – it's very funny and one never tires of it. Fancy watching? It'll be fabulous on a large screen. And it's in the original language!'

'Is it a comedy?' my mother asked.

'No, far better than that: it's a Noh play.'

'A *what* play?' my father asked, looking up from his crossword book.

'Let me explain. Noh, or Gagaku, if you prefer. Or even Bugaku, if you're really punctilious about terms. Are you a connoisseur?'

'No, I'm not,' my father replied. 'I was merely enquiring. To be frank, I'd just like to bring today to a peaceful conclusion.'

Outside, sleet was beginning to fall. There was still a long way to go.

'You're going to love this!' said Edouard, sliding the DVD into the player. 'We're going to be rolling in the aisles! If there's something you don't understand—'

'We'll let you explain,' my mother completed his sentence. 'Absolutely.'

A man appeared suddenly on screen dressed in a black satin kimono secured with a broad red belt. He was alone on a vast, empty stage and he glanced to left and right, as if he were searching for something. His eyebrows above two black made-up eyes gave him a furious, menacing air. All of a sudden he froze, let out a little high-pitched cry and started to quiver from head to toe like a reed in a storm.

'He's angry now, isn't he?' I asked Edouard.

'No, he's extremely happy. He's a joker, someone who looks on the bright side of life.'

Soon afterwards the man took a big step forward and brought his foot down hard on the floor, producing a sound like thunder. Then he rolled his eyes, wiggled his ears, made his jaw crack, wobbled his backside, inflated his stomach as far as he could, pushed out his belly button towards the sky, touched the end of his nose with his tongue and finally let out a roar that made us all jump.

'Poor man!' said Edouard.

'What do you mean, poor man?' my father exclaimed with surprise.

'You can see that he's sad. What, you can't?'

'Oh yes, now you mention it.'

'Watch out! Watch out now!' said Edouard, pointing his finger at the screen. 'Concentrate, by golly, or you'll miss the best bit!'

The man, who was still alone on stage, started to gaze up into the air. His upturned face seemed to be following invisible clouds. He raised a forefinger as if to test the direction of the wind.

And at this point Edouard burst out laughing. 'Ha ha, that's such a great joke, isn't it? I crack up every time I watch this scene. You can see why, can't you?'

'Priceless,' my father muttered.

'It really is. Oh, I have an idea: why don't we watch that again? Just for fun!'

'No,' my father shot back. 'It'll interrupt the flow.'

'You're right. OK, watch out – more action coming up!'

As if on cue, a dainty figure stepped out from the wings. She was shrouded in vaporous clouds, which made her look as if she had wings. She padded silently towards the man in the dark robe, but he didn't appear to notice her presence. She circled him for around twenty minutes.

She vanished, and the man collapsed until he lay flat as a pancake on the floor.

'It fools me every time!' Edouard cried. 'Admit that the ending comes as a complete surprise!'

'I do admit that ... hee hee, what a massive surprise! You expect anything but that to happen! Is that really the end? Are you sure?'

'Of the first part, yes. There are fifteen altogether. It's a guaranteed hit: action, laughter, romance. If you'd like, I can come back tomorrow and ...'

Outside, the sleet had turned to rain. My thoughts turned to Napoleon. And Alexandre, without his cap.

Mum had nodded off and her hand was lying slackly on the armrest of her chair. Her sketchbook had fallen onto the carpet.

At that exact moment I felt the passing of time.

Edouard had left a long time ago, otter on his head and yak hair on his feet, when Josephine suddenly re-emerged in the early evening, looking rested and well.

My father told her about Edouard's visit. She stretched, yawned and asked, 'And what did he want?'

'He came about the marriage.'

'Marriage?' Josephine gasped. 'What marriage?'

'His.'

'Oh? He's getting married?'

'Um, yes.'

'Hang on, he could have told me. To whom?'

'To you!'

Josephine spun around smartly.

'To *me*?'

'Yes, because you agreed. You even told him so on the phone yesterday.'

Josephine let herself topple backwards onto the sofa and shut her eyes, presumably searching her memory.

'By the way, he's a nice guy. A bit weird, but nice.'

'Be quiet,' said Josephine. 'I'm trying to remember. Yes, I can sense the fog clearing . . . It's slowly coming back. He must have found it very strange.'

'When?'

'When you told him I was drunk. And already taken. Taken by Sunshine.'

My father bit his lip, and my mother gave a snort. Josephine got to her feet.

'Wait a minute, you don't mean to say—'

'Oh, come on, Mum. Remember: "ready for a new life". You wanted to go with him to Patagonia.'

Josephine clasped her head in her hands and began to rock back and forth. 'I don't believe it. I can't believe it. It was merely a figure of speech! I mean, it was a Christmas wish. You'd have to be as thick as two short planks not to get that.'

'I really don't understand what's going on inside that head of yours,' he murmured. 'You said you wanted a fresh start, a new lease of life now that your jumper is finished. Off to Patagonia! That guy turns up in his fur cap, all dressed up in yak hair from his toes to his nostrils, banging on about Go plays and games of Noh . . . So I—'

'The other way round, I think, Dad,' I said. 'Noh plays and games of Go. Would you like me to explain them to you?'

'I couldn't give a damn!' he yelled. 'I don't give one stinking damn! I don't understand a thing about the game or the plays or anything else that's going on.' He muttered to himself for a few seconds before launching into another angry tirade. 'No, I don't understand all this stuff about marriage, divorce, a fresh start and sharing eternity like a baguette at a picnic, either. And the last thing I want is an explanation!'

All the while Josephine had been moping in the corner with her head in her hands. 'What am I going to do? How do I get out of this? I want to go back to my Sunshine. I have absolutely no desire to go to Asia.'

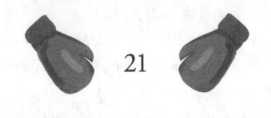

21

The following night was pretty much like most of my other nights. The trees continued to fall. They were all gigantic, broad and knotty. Oddly, though, the height and width of their trunks and the spread of their branches suggested frailty rather than strength. The more imposing they looked, the more fragile they actually were.

Alexandre Rawcziik, Endov and I were walking over a scattering of dry, dead leaves that made no sound, as if we were moving without actually touching the ground. In my dream, we proceeded from tree to tree, checking that they were OK and not under any sort of threat, but no sooner had we touched them than the danger became apparent.

Alexandre's cap was huge, almost as tall as the trees. I took a few steps backwards. I looked up, but all I could see was the cap and a curtain of dense foliage blocking out the sky. Soon the trees began to sway from left to right, and the roots broke free of the soil with a deep growling sound. Alexandre was lost.

The trees crashed to the ground, and behind them emerged even greater trees, more majestic and emperor-like trees, but they too came crashing down. I woke up and began to weep.

In the dark the phone began to ring. Dad and Mum jumped out of bed. I joined them in the living room. Josephine wasn't awake yet.

Napoleon. It had to be him.

'It's a paramedic,' my father told us, covering the mouth-piece with one hand.

My mother asked me to go back to bed, but I stayed on the bottom step. My father repeated what the paramedic had told him so that my mother could follow the conversation.

'A fire?'

Silence.

'I see. He started ironing but went off to the bowling alley in his underpants, with Endov trailing behind him, leaving the iron smouldering on his shirt. Yes, no doubt about it – that's him.'

Silence.

'What did you say to him? He's being difficult? Sounds right, yes. Join the club! Not funny? No, you're right. But, you know, sometimes, if you don't laugh . . .'

Silence.

'He can't remember anything and claims that you set the house on fire to deport him. And that you and I are working together?' My father continued for my mother's benefit.

Silence.

'OK, well it's not the first time. Locked in the toilet with the dog where he's yelling the lyrics to that "Barracuda" song. He's rambling on about a guy called Rocky? He says no one's ever appreciated Rocky's legacy? I hope you're specially trained to deal with temperamental former boxers, because otherwise you're not going to get much sleep tonight. That isn't funny either? OK, put him on.'

Silence.

'What? He refuses to talk to me? He called me a . . . And you think that's funny? Makes you laugh, does it? No, I'm not laughing.'

Silence.

'He says the empire is under threat and he will talk only to his major general? Yes, I know who he means. An immediate meeting of the chiefs of staff?'

We woke Josephine in the middle of the night. My father claimed that the bank – where he worked – had been robbed and he had to return home as a matter of urgency. She came outside with us and sat perched on the front steps in her dressing gown, lit by the headlights of our car. We all had to leave and waved goodbye to her.

My father drove like a man possessed. The car forged through the night. I fell asleep and woke up again with a start. I felt oddly at ease, hoping that this journey would last for ever.

I accompanied my father into the service stations whenever he wanted to have a break or a cup of coffee to keep him awake. In one of those places, in the early hours of the morning – we had roughly sixty miles left to go – he smashed up a vending machine that had swallowed his coin without giving anything in return. Two musclemen arrived wearing armbands saying 'Security' around their biceps; the word seemed more threatening than anything else.

One of the two said to my father, 'Making trouble here, little man?'

They started to argue, and I thought a fight was going to break out. My father began to bob about on his feet with his fists raised in front of his chin. The two men watched him with mocking smiles. I grabbed my father's arm.

'Come on, Dad. They have no idea about boxing.'

'You're right. They know nothing!'

Then, as the sliding door was opening to let us out of the service station, my father turned to face the two guards. 'WET BLANKETS!' he shouted.

We ran as fast as our legs would carry us to the car and drove off at high speed.

We turned off the motorway and, just before we arrived, my father slammed on the brakes to avoid hitting a white doe that was standing motionless in the middle of the road, staring at us with its gentle eyes. It took several seconds for the graceful creature to cross the road. My mother's words at the bowling alley – 'All that is fragile is beautiful' – echoed in my mind.

Finally, we reached our destination. 'Over to you!' my father told me as he pulled up outside Napoleon's house.

I went inside to find the paramedic still there, wrapped up asleep in a chequered blanket next to a cup of cold coffee. The smell of burning hung around the house, and the kitchen was as black as coal. Endov waddled slowly towards me, fixing me with a bemused gaze. The dog looked as if he knew an awful lot. He lay down on his side. We would have to take him back to our house, since Napoleon wouldn't be able to take care of him any longer.

'I'm the major general,' I told the paramedic.

'What a weird army,' he replied.

As soon as I caught sight of him I felt something I'd rather not have felt: Napoleon struck me as old. Before me was a very elderly gentleman, and I was gripped by the same anxiety that had taken hold of me in my dream. There was a force threatening to topple us.

For a few minutes I had the impression that I was invisible. I realised that my grandfather didn't really recognise me. His eyes appeared to be searching my face for a reminder of someone he might have encountered before – someone whose name he had since forgotten.

I could hear a tap dripping continually in the background. Each droplet splashed against the ceramic sink.

It was as if these drips were measuring time. All of a sudden, Napoleon signalled to me to come closer and whispered in my ear, 'Don't tell anyone, but I've hidden the Camembert.'

Noticing my bewilderment, he added, 'That ambulance man . . . He came looking for the Camembert. But luckily I saw straight through his ploy. You should've seen his face when he opened the fridge. He almost ate his hat! Go and have a look.'

He followed me into the kitchen, his eyes gleaming with triumphant anticipation. The room was unrecognisable with its soot-covered walls, and the pungent odour of burnt Formica. It almost made me retch. I opened the fridge and an involuntary smile came to my lips. I turned to my grandfather.

'Why have you put all your underpants in the fridge? And why do you have so many?'

There were at least a hundred pairs in there, all impeccably folded and arranged.

Had he heard my question? He gazed up at the ceiling, his brow furrowed, and muttered, 'It could do with a good lick of paint in here.'

'Hey, why are your pants in there?' I repeated.

'Why?' he answered. 'To piss her off, that's why.'

'Who? I don't understand.'

He burst out laughing. 'Who? You're a right joker. Are you losing your marbles? You know full well who. Madame Taillandec.'

I'd heard that name before. Madame Taillandec had been his primary school teacher, and he'd talked about her with a mixture of resentment and affection.

'You put your underpants in the fridge to piss Madame Taillandec off?'

'That's right. Her and the ambulance man. Actually, you see – and don't you go repeating this – the ambulance man is her son ... Her secret son. She's a swindler. They're conspiring. Together they were trying to steal my Camembert. Ha ha, there are no flies on me, though, and I hid it! Instead of cheese they found pants. Pretty smart, eh!' He pointed to his temple.

The tap dripped in the background.

All of a sudden, in the space of a couple of seconds, he seemed to revert to his old self.

'Oh, there you are, pal. I was expecting you. Wow, that's some cap you've got there.'

'Thanks, Grandpa.'

'Don't call me that! Have you seen this place? I've no idea what happened. Have you?'

'No.'

'A short circuit, maybe?'

'Maybe.'

'You know, it's funny, but lots of things came back to me

last night. I really do have a cast-iron brain. Everything's stored away in here.' He tapped his fist against his skull before asking me, 'When's your birthday again?'

'You've forgotten?'

'Not really forgotten. More like a slight doubt.'

'In May,' I said. 'The eighteenth.'

'In May, the eighteenth,' he repeated quietly. 'That's right.'

He appeared to be considering something and doing complicated calculations. He suddenly came alive. 'By the way, about Operation Taxi, the mission I gave you. You know, the beach where—'

'Yes, my emperor, I know exactly where it is. A little town called Houlgate.'

'Ah, that's it. That's the one. I remembered everything else about it. Houl-gate. Sounds like caramel melting in your mouth. Actually, the beach wasn't *that* small.'

His relief was obvious. I silently swore to do my very best never to forget the name of that beach.

'I'm going to give you a job to do, pal. Go into the basement. To the shelves where the gloves, the bag and the other stuff are.'

'OK, I know the place.'

'You'll find a jar of magnesium – you know, the white powder you put on your hands to stop them from getting hurt.'

'All right.'

He burst out laughing. 'Except it isn't magnesium! Hee

hee! It was a ruse to make sure Josephine wouldn't go sticking her nose in the basement.'

Within a few minutes I returned with the jar, which Napoleon opened immediately.

'Get a whiff of that,' he said. 'Just a little sniff.'

The scent of a beach. The same sand that Josephine had. The same gentle, faded fragrance of the past, which conjured up images of Napoleon and Josephine walking along that shore. I couldn't help but imagine the imprint of their toes in the sand.

'Don't tell a soul, OK. Top secret. I have my dignity. Later, as my major general, you'll be in charge of protecting the relics of my empire.'

He put the lid back on the jar and screwed it tight with all his strength.

A letter from Grandma

My darling boy,

I was sad when you rushed off the other day, it's
important to say goodbye, especially as I was
completely unlike myself on Christmas Eve. I . . .
what's the expression you kids use nowadays? Lost
it, I think, in any case the next day the bubbles had
sunk back down into my knees, it was raining, it
was my first Christmas without Napoleon. Edouard
rang back, wanting to talk to me about the future,
but it was bad timing because I only wanted to hear
about the past.

However, we did meet in a tearoom, but he didn't
really know how to bring up the subject of marriage,
the nincompoop, it was obvious, he kept rocking
from one buttock to the other as if he needed a wee,
but it was quite endearing and above all it suited
me because I didn't know how to respond. A flat
no seemed a little cruel. Anyway, I didn't feel like
answering his questions or even chatting to him. So I

suggested what people always suggest when they have nothing to say to each other – go to the cinema. I don't know what we'd do without it.

I felt like seeing a comedy and he said that there was a really good, entertaining film by a certain Kurosawa called *Seven Samurai*. I didn't understand a thing, not a single thing, first of all the film was in black and white. It took place a long time ago when people didn't used to smile very much and it lasted for exactly 207 minutes because we were lucky enough, according to Edouard, to see the long version. He'd seen the short version 6 times, luckily there were only 7 samurais because if there'd been 20 we'd have spent two days at the cinema. There was one who looked a bit like Edouard and during the closing titles he (Ed, not the samurai) asked me what I'd thought of it, so to improve the mood I said I thought it was sam-all-right, but that didn't amuse him one bit. He gave me a stern look, he even said that I was showing no respect for an ancient culture, that I was like a pirate towards things of the mind and that this was a serious difference between him and me, but after 207 minutes of Japanese brawling I felt entitled to make a pun, even if it was a lame one. But that's the problem with Edouard: he takes everything so seriously, well, one of the problems. The second is that he isn't Napoleon. I started sulking, like a little girl. After 15 minutes of this it was obvious that we were fighting like cat and dog, and that's when he said, 'But my word, my dear Josephine, we're arguing. How charming!'

In a sense I was glad to get out of discussing marriage. I had no idea how to present the situation or how to explain that I couldn't stop thinking about Napoleon like an infatuated teenager, especially when we touched the sand and looked at the map. Don't tell him about this, Napoleon's not the kind to watch samurais, but he's full of the same kinds of devilry as them.

Eduardo finally calmed down and changed the subject. I don't think he really wanted to be tied down either, he said he didn't want to waste any more time cooking or cleaning and he was going to look for an assistant who could help him out with his daily chores, He looked at me with some regret in his eyes, in fact he left me there, just like that, without warning, with the excuse that he needed to take care of the matter and make a few phone calls to find a suitable person, so I walked home by myself along the lake with a hint of sadness in my heart.

It's hard because in spite of the samurais, his otter-skin hat and the yak hairs, Edouard is a very gentle, very kind man and I wonder if I'm not missing out on something. Napoleon or Edouard? It was funny to imagine Napoleon and Edouard on opposite sides of a set of scales, which tilted first one way and then the other. It made me laugh; it's pretty peculiar to have these kinds of problems at my age. Out on the lake a family of swans was moving along in a triangle, leaving a small wake behind them. Night was falling and a wave of grief hit me. All of this is Napoleon's fault, of course. I feel ashamed asking, but I would like to know how he is and how far he's got in his new life. He's proud and even if it kills him he won't admit it, but say what you like, Napoleon's been the only sun in my life and even now that he's a setting sun, he still keeps me warm, When I think back, I can feel the sand under my feet and I can hear the waves, exactly as they were back then. You see, time doesn't pass, that's what you figure out as you get old. Honestly, my darling, matters of the heart are so complicated, too complicated. The worst thing is that the older you get the less you understand about them, if we could choose, well I think it'd be better to steer well clear of love, I'm going to go back to my knitting, like that dumb cluck Penelope.

Big kisses from your grandma

22

And so, my emperor's final battle began. An unequal battle.
His foe was elusive. This time he knew where to strike and
his aim was good. At the body, the head, the heart: he knew
which blows hurt, discouraged and humiliated. The opponent was a master of every aspect of the game. He knew how
to dodge and feint and he gave Napoleon no respite. Night
and day, my embattled emperor suffered one humiliation
after another. He was forced onto one knee but he always
got up again – once, twice, a dozen times. His adversary's
technique was inspired by thousands of years of practice.
He attacked the body by causing Napoleon's muscles to
melt away; he attacked his mind by shattering his memory.

He was a devious monster, adept at toying with his poor
prey and giving him false hopes, only to dash them. His foe
was like a wild beast with gleaming eyes, a hyena who would

occasionally disappear back into the bush only to observe us better. Sometimes, I felt as if the Napoleon of old had returned. Some days his face was calm, his remarks scathing.

'They're not going to deport me anytime soon! How about we go bowling, pal?'

'That'd be great, my emperor,' I would reply with tears in my eyes.

'So why are you blubbing if it'd be so great? Oh, I see. You have instructions? Is that it, pal?' His face was full of rage, but there were also hints of a smile and affection in his eyes. 'Even my general's deserting me!' he said in his reedy voice.

I hung my head. My father had asked me to let him know if I found the house empty or if Napoleon tried to get in his car. Dad had hired a woman to spend several hours a day with him, a very softly spoken lady whom Napoleon alternately mistook for Josephine, a summer camp group leader, the postwoman or even his mother. A lady so discreet that she blended into the faded wallpaper of the corridor.

'All right, it's true,' he said one day. 'I admit I have the occasional memory lapse. Nothing to make a fuss about, though. It might be too late for circumnavigating the globe and that's no problem, but for everything else . . . I still have strength in reserve. We have our whole lives ahead of us.'

'The empire will merely be a little smaller, my emperor.'

'That's right, pal. Well put. The main thing is to reign, whatever the size of the realm. Come over here.'

Arm-wrestle. What used to be a special moment petrified

me now. I was the one who gritted his teeth and resisted, the one who was ready to throw in the towel. My hand slammed down on the table. Did he believe me? Was he pretending? Why did his victories wring no more than a strained smile from his lips?

Such scenes were followed by periods of dejection, when I could see from the look in his eyes that he didn't recognise me. In these moments I whispered gently to him, 'But, my emperor, it's me, your major general! Your pal. We have an empire to defend. The borders are under attack!'

No use. His stupid smile didn't change, his shoulders still drooped.

'Your major general! Your pal!' I repeated with disbelief.

'I think you must be mistaken, young man. I'm not an emperor, and I've never had a major general.'

I fetched Rocky's portrait.

'And this, Grandpa, is Rocky. The boxer who gave you everything.'

In his moments of confusion, the only thing that seemed to liberate him from his struggles against the erasing of memories was the picture of Rocky. He smiled so lovingly as he ran his fingers over Rocky's sweaty face, and tears would well up in my eyes. Napoleon didn't fully recognise him and seemed to be trying to figure out to which part of his life the man in the photo belonged. With a sigh, he gave up.

'Don't forget to take your dog with you when you leave. I'm allergic to dog hair.'

I was a general without an emperor. One day, when I was feeling disheartened, I came up with the idea of opening the little jar of sand. Napoleon looked at me with surprise.

'I found it odd enough that you were claiming to be my general, but you also have some very strange habits. Do I really have to smell that sand?'

'Yes, my emperor.'

'I hope you're not making me sniff crap.'

He closed his eyes and sniffed. Aromas of yesteryear seemed to blaze a trail through his foggy memory.

'Oh, that does remind me of something. I don't know quite what, but . . . Can I have another sniff?'

I nodded.

'Oh yes. What a wonderful fragrance!'

'It's the sand from Josephine's beach, my emperor. You don't remember? The little beach . . . Emperor . . . '

'Stop calling me by that stupid title. Do I look like an emperor to you? Why not call me Grandpa while you're at it? To be honest, I can't understand why you're here. I do feel that we've met before somewhere, though. Or else you look a little like someone I once knew.'

The phone rang in the middle of the following night. It was the director of a service station near Évreux. Napoleon had filled up his tank with diesel by mistake and the Peugeot 404 hadn't taken it well. It was a good thing my father had

had the foresight to slip our phone number into the 404's glove compartment.

'Évreux?' my father said quizzically as he got dressed. 'Good grief! Why Normandy? Do you know, Leonard?'

'No, Dad, I don't.'

'Is there a boxing gym in Évreux?'

During this period, I'd convinced my parents to let me leave school at lunchtime so I could go and enjoy half an hour's respite and reverie with Napoleon while we listened to his favourite quiz show. It was a blissful thirty minutes during which I would see him at his pugnacious best, displaying the same biting wit and a memory as sharp as a tack. I only wish I could have brought Endov with me, but there wasn't enough time to go home first, and I couldn't allow the dog to come to school with me, no matter how much I wanted him to.

'Another question,' the presenter announced. 'Concentrate now. One of Victor Hugo's daughters went mad. What was her name?'

Whispers from the two contestants as they consulted for a few seconds.

'Hugo!' said one of them.

'No, her first name.'

'Oh, that makes it much harder!'

More muted mumblings: 'Mmm, mmmm ... No, yes, maybe ... That's got to be it!'

'We're going to go for it. Victorine!'

'No,' said What's-his-face.

'Oh. In that case, Huguette?'

'No.'

'Marcelline?'

'Don't be so stupid!' Napoleon interjected. 'Adèle.'

'Are you sure?' I asked him.

'Absolutely. That guy deserves a kick in the pants, not the jackpot!' Where, having never opened a book in his life, had Napoleon heard about Victor Hugo's daughter? Today there was no hesitation, he answered every question immediately.

'The capital of Mongolia? Ulan Bator.'

'In which film does Gary Cooper play Link Jones? *Man of the West*, obviously. From 1958. They really must think we're thick.'

'*Asterias*? Starfish, you daft idiot! Everyone knows that!'

When I switched off the radio, it felt as if I were switching off my emperor's mind too, as if without the presenter's voice and the applause of the well-behaved audience he was no longer connected to our world.

'Game over,' he would say. 'Now for serious matters.'

What did he mean by that?

I had to go back to school, leaving him there alone with his lurking foe. I closed the door behind me.

As soon as we had got home from Josephine's, I had returned Alexandre's cap and presented him with my mother's drawing. He seemed almost unsurprised to find his headgear mended and simply placed it on his head. He examined the sketch at length before slipping it carefully into his schoolbag.

'I'll keep it for the rest of my life' was all he said. 'Your mother is a true artist. You're lucky. Only artists can make things last for ever.'

I could feel that his heart was fit to burst, even if he couldn't express himself properly.

In the following weeks he walked me part of the way home and each time I wanted to ask about the initials emblazoned on his famous cap – R.R. – but I didn't want to pry and risk being rejected.

One day I invited him to our house.

'I have to get home,' he said curtly as he slowly backed away from our house.

He seemed to be trapped inside some kind of secret as if it were a prison, so I told myself that he alone could decide when he wanted to share his story, even if that moment might never come.

My mother often left her sketchbooks lying around. One evening I noticed that one of them contained sketches of a kind I'd never seen her draw before. All sorts of insects. They were only vague outlines, hurried sketches, but as with every time my mother got into a new subject, there were dozens of them.

I questioned her about them. She confessed that she'd bumped into Alexandre one evening. She'd recognised him by his amazing cap and, like me, she had been drawn into conversation with him. He had talked about insects and she was captivated and touched by his devotion to trying to protect these tiny creepy-crawlies which most other people just tended to squash by accident. She'd immediately got out her newly purchased pencils.

She had listened to him spouting information about the Chinese bruchid, the Capricorn beetle and *Carabus auronitens*.

'He was as fragile as the insects he was protecting,' she said, adding, 'There's poetry everywhere we look – even in the dust.'

My mother was right. That same poetry might even have inspired Napoleon's night-time escapades. These adventures with my father were so unexpected, and our pursuits so bizarre, that I sometimes found it hard to believe they had actually happened. Anyone but Alexandre would have refused to believe anything I said, mocking me or simply disregarding me completely. He looked forward so impatiently to my stories, greeting them with such obvious enthusiasm that through his eyes my grandfather became an unforgettable epic hero.

'That's a great story! Take a marble. No, two!'

*

That spring, the phone often rang in the middle of the night. I'd come to anticipate the calls. I would go to bed fully dressed. It was never long before I heard my dad's hurried footsteps and Endov's barking. He would burst into my room, his face a mask of concern.

'Let's go. It's quite a drive.'

Boxing gyms, trunk road lay-bys, deserted service stations, twenty-four-hour fast-food joints: Napoleon showed us all of them. Once we were called by a driver who'd picked him up hitchhiking; another time it was the manager of a service station; a lorry driver in whose cab Napoleon had fallen asleep; a toll-booth assistant; a farmer who'd found my grandfather astride one of his cows; the trainer at a boxing gym in a tiny Parisian street; a station master who'd discovered him in a waiting room or the conductor of a train whose emergency cord my grandfather had pulled. How did he get so far? It was a mystery. Napoleon didn't always recognise us and one evening he even mistook my father for his old trainer, Jojo Lagrange.

'I've lost my gloves, Jojo!' he said, gazing at his bony little fists.

At other times things went less smoothly, and Napoleon would play to the gallery in the middle of the night by screaming that he was being kidnapped. My father would have to justify his actions to crowds of nocturnal vigilantes (lorry drivers, bikers, touring basketball teams) who regarded these spectacular altercations as entertainment.

'I swear he's my father!' my father declared in his own defence.

'No way,' yelled Napoleon. 'He isn't my son. You're wrong. Everyone's wrong.'

These desperate words, 'I swear he's not my son', still seem to reverberate in the streets on dark nights.

Having dispersed the spectators who had taken Napoleon's side, we had to work as a team to calm him down and usher him into the car where he would grumble for the first few miles before falling asleep. He looked tiny, hunched up on the back seat.

Occasionally Napoleon would suddenly regain his grip on reality, as if he were re-emerging from a deep dream.

He would ask me, 'What am I doing *here*, pal?'

'You ran away, my emperor. You are one hell of a barracuda.'

'"Barracuda ... "' he would sing to the tune of the Claude François song.

He gestured at my father. 'We'll wear him down, won't we?'

'We sure will, my emperor!' I replied.

'What did he say?' my father asked.

'Oh, nothing. Only that he's happy you came.'

In recent times, barely a week had passed without Napoleon getting into mischief, and, although I dreaded the sound of the phone ringing in the middle of the night, I was also glad for the opportunity to rescue my emperor.

My father and I would sometimes stop at a rundown late-night roadside café to have a coffee and ask for directions. These surreal places made him talkative, and he would end up confiding his uncertainty to me.

'Sometimes I wonder about boxing and Napoleon ... I have my doubts.'

Yes, the idea had crossed my mind, too, but I had always dismissed it as sacrilegious. Of course there were all the photos, but they were of a young man fighting. A young man who looked nothing like the old man I knew. Like Rocky, he had fought under a pseudonym, and not one article mentioned our surname, Sunshine.

How could we know if Napoleon's empire was not in fact just a great pyramid of paper and lies? Who could we ask now? Josephine? She'd never seen him box, having met him when he'd started his second life as a taxi driver, and, in reality, she knew little more than we did.

23

One Saturday morning I found a nice notebook on my desk – my mother's drawings bound with thread into an album. The title on the front page was:

The Book of Napoleon

I was tempted to flick through it straight away, but I eventually got up and climbed the stairs to my mother's studio. No one there. No one in the kitchen either, but I did find a note. My parents had had to go out, but I wasn't to worry.

I hurriedly got dressed and ran over to Napoleon's house. He was obviously waiting for me. Freshly shaven, his white hair carefully combed back, he was wearing the same white suit he'd worn on the evening we went bowling with my parents. He was on top form. It was as if the enemy had retreated. Placed in the middle of the living room was a small suitcase and the black bowling ball.

'Ah, there you are. I was waiting for you. Nice weather, eh?' His voice was clear and steady. He noticed that my gaze had been drawn to his suitcase. 'Don't worry about the suitcase. I was intending to take a short break, but we're actually going to do something else now. Open the French windows, pal.'

Looking out over the untended garden, we breathed in deeply, filling our lungs.

'Ah, spring!' he said. 'There's nothing quite like spring, pal. Especially the springtime of your life.'

I smiled. So did he.

'My pal,' he said. 'I have no idea how much longer we have ahead of us. So let's not waste any time!'

He pointed to the album tucked under my arm.

'What's that you've got there? Let me have a little look. Not too much writing, I hope?'

'No. Just pictures,' I said, holding out the book.

'Because I don't feel like racking my brains, you see. Not today. They're quite racked enough as it is!' He burst out laughing. Little tears seeped out of the corners of his eyes. 'Now what do we have here ... A beautiful album. Is this a present?

'Correct. A *sort* of present. *The Book of Napoleon*. For your birthday.'

'That's a long way off but you're right – you never know

what might happen. It's better to think ahead. Always stay one step ahead of your opponent.'

Our eyes met fleetingly. His face took on a serious expression, and his fingers began to turn the pages of the album. My mother's drawings were in chronological order, and each one left its impression on Napoleon's features. The last fight against Rocky; his first encounter with Josephine in the taxi; their footprints in the wet sand on the beach; the scandal with the fluorescent tie; his black ball striking the white pins; Endov as my faithful companion; my father shadow-boxing in the kitchen; my father's head as an eleventh skittle.

Napoleon screwed up his eyes in amusement, smiled affectionately and let his mouth fall open in amazement. He saw Josephine giving him a friendly wave from her garden and waved back, mouthing words I didn't understand.

'Oh, give me a break,' he said, 'I'm not really going to start blubbing, am I? I'm going soft.'

My mother had only drawn herself once. She was sitting beside Napoleon opposite a man in a white coat. A kindly yet mournful atmosphere hung over the three figures.

Intrigued, I asked, 'Where was this?'

'Oh, it was no big deal, pal. Just a charming little outing with your mother a few months back. We had a fine time. If I'm ever reincarnated, I'd like to come back as one of her pencils.'

It was a hospital visit, I was sure. Just before the divorce.

The final pages of the album were as white as the walls of the hospital in the picture. It was Napoleon's job to fill them.

'Enough reading,' he suddenly announced. 'Time for some action.' He put on his leather jacket, just as before. 'We're going to cut and run. Get your skates on, pal. All aboard the 404!' He noticed my reluctance. 'Come on – one last trick.'

The same old signs of kindness and protectiveness, stretching an arm out in front of me whenever he stepped on the brakes, a reflex from before the era of proper seat-belts. After driving through three red lights and ignoring five Give Way signs, he ground to a halt in front of a hair-dresser's salon where there was just about enough room to park a scooter.

'Isn't that space a little small, my emperor?' I commented.

'No, not if we ask nicely.'

Crunch against the car behind, crunch against the one in front, two mangled bumpers and the Peugeot 404 was just about well parked.

'See, pal? Loads of room! They can take away my licence if they want. I don't care – I don't have one!'

His parking manoeuvres were greeted with a chorus of beeping horns.

'Any of you fancy my fist in your face?' he yelled out of the window. 'You barbarians! Ah, there's nothing like a good outburst to make you feel young again!'

I had brought Napoleon's wheelchair as a precaution,

and he shifted himself into it. He was now using it more than ever since his back injury and sometimes my dad and I would take it with us to wherever we had to collect him. He pointed to the hairdresser's.

'Going to get your hair cut?' I asked.

'I just want to be more or less presentable. First impressions count.'

We entered the shop. From my vantage point on a chair at the back of the hairdresser's, I watched clumps of hair fall to the floor like snowflakes. I felt a desperate urge to pick one up, but I didn't dare. Our eyes met in the mirror every now and then. At last, the hairdresser held up a small mirror to the back of my grandfather's head.

'How does that look?' he asked.

'Perfect. What do you reckon, pal?'

'You look magnificent.'

'What about your 'burns?' the hairdresser asked.

'Come on, baby, light my fire,' Napoleon replied, and they burst out laughing in unison.

Outside on the pavement he hesitated. 'I don't want to go home, pal. Let's go for a drink! It'll be harder afterwards.'

'When, afterwards?'

'Just afterwards. Anyway, I have something to tell you.'

My heart was pounding. For some weeks now I had been feeling that every time with Napoleon was the last time.

The café was crawling with people. Young people, old people, families, loners and everyone else seemed to have decided to meet up there, and Napoleon snagged his wheel-chair on various prams and scooters.

'Having a Coke, pal?'

I smiled and nodded.

'Two Cokes!' he ordered at the top of his voice, snapping his fingers.

He scanned the other customers. There was a hint of tiredness in his eyes that I'd got used to seeing. How much longer until the mist would descend? Quarter of an hour? Half an hour? It was impossible to tell.

'Remember when I was at the hospital, pal? For my back injury. You do? I wondered why people couldn't sit still. Always travelling this way or that. Never spending more than five minutes in the same place.'

'I remember.'

The waiter set down two glasses of Coke in front of us. Napoleon pulled a fifty-euro note from his pocket.

'Keep the change. Anyway, today I came up with the answer.'

He looked at me proudly. I was a little disappointed. I'd thought I was about to learn Napoleon's secret and now . . .

'Yes, I have the answer, and it's incredibly simple. Because they're bored, that's why. And when you're bored, bad thoughts pop into your head. One bad thought in par-ticular. That's why we're always out and about. To avoid thinking, to escape from that thought.'

'Which thought do you mean?'

He tore the wrapping from one end of his straw, then blew into it, sending the paper sailing away over the other tables. The tiny rocket glided for a few seconds before crash-landing in a woman's hair. She didn't notice.

'You see,' said Napoleon, 'I'm eighty-six years old. I don't look it, admittedly, but I am.'

'Yes.'

'Translate that into the number of football World Cups I've lived through. Go on, it's instructive. Do the sum on the tablecloth . . . Show me. That's right.'

'Twenty-one point five.'

His lifetime reduced to a paltry span of fewer than twenty-two World Cups. And then the final whistle.

'Makes you think, eh?'

My chest was shaken by sobs. The noise around us thickened into a dense blanket that smothered me. The sound of glasses clinking on the counter were like nails being hammered into my head. I felt like abandoning my emperor to his own devices.

'Anyway, pal, time's running out. The meter's always running. I've got something else to tell you. Something more important. Are you ready? You are? A secret . . . '

He paused and scanned my face for signs of encouragement.

'I won't tell anyone.'

'Mum's the word?'

'My lips are sealed.'

He glanced left and right, as if someone might be spying on us. He looked like a frightened bird.

'Well, pal, here goes. I can deal with numbers, but the rest ... I ... I ...' He took a deep breath and in one burst said, 'Icannotread. There, I've said it. And, boy, does it feel good.'

'Can't read? You mean ...'

'Can't read, full stop. Or write, logically. It isn't very hard to understand. Not a single word. Nothing.'

He pointed to a poster for a major horse-riding event on the wall. 'That poster over there, for example. Can't make head nor tail of it. All I see is a nag. I've never learned. It soon got on my nerves and I always cheated. My whole life. Even Madame Taillandec was completely fooled.'

I thought of Josephine, but he got there first. 'She never guessed. As you can imagine, I never dared tell her. Especially as she asked me on the day we met in my taxi if I liked the novels of some writer or other, and I said yes, I loved them. That's how it started. You tell a lie and soon you're trapped in your own lies. I've never understood how letters, signs, accents and everything are organised. What you need to be able to read as a boxer is the fear and doubt in your opponent's eyes, and you won't find that in any book.'

'But how did you get by as a taxi driver?'

'I followed my instincts.'

'Wow, you're amazing. The emperor of tricksters.'

'Thanks, pal. Know how old your father was when he learned to read? Four. He learned to read at the age of four.

I offered to take him to watch a fight but he preferred to read a book. Little brat. Before he could read he wanted me to read him stories. Every day. I chose a book at random and made up something to fit the pictures. He always fell for it!'

He gave a mischievous cackle of self-satisfaction and beckoned me closer.

'Listen to me, pal, because I can tell you: I want to learn.'

'To read?' I whispered.

'Yes, my general. To read, not to sew. But I don't know if the enemy will give us enough time. It'll be my final conquest! I know I won't be able to make much use of my knowledge but, still, it could come in handy. Maybe they ask you to fill in forms up above!'

I hung my head. The hairdresser. *I just want to be more or less presentable. First impressions count.* The suitcase in the middle of the living room. Our eyes met and I saw the resignation in his: he'd agreed to leave his house.

'Don't think of it as a surrender, pal, or even a retreat. Merely a decoy tactic. We lull the enemy; we deceive him.'

'We trick him.'

'That's right, we trick him. You've got it. And no blubbing or he'll pounce. By the way, I have a plan. Got a pen and paper?'

He saw the amazement in my eyes.

'I'm going to dictate my conditions,' he said. 'I'm worried I'll forget them otherwise, you see.'

I let my biro run across the paper, taking down nothing

but the words he spoke. Occasionally he'd stress something, adding, 'Underline that. It's very important.'

I filled an entire sheet. Napoleon seemed relieved.

'Your emperor will fight to the bitter end. He won't give an inch. And we'll keep in touch, OK?'

'Yes, my emperor. We'll keep in touch. Always.'

'How strange, I feel cold. Shall we go home?'

The irritating dripping of the tap continued to mark the passing of time. I had the impression that each drop made a louder splash against the ceramic sink than the last. I felt like aiming a kick at the small suitcase in the centre of the room. Napoleon studied his house as if seeing it for the first time.

'My emperor . . .'

He jumped. My gaze met his. His blue eyes could only scour his thicket of memories where the past and the present were entangled like vines in the jungle.

'Listen to this, Grandpa. *Three drops on china. A tree beyond glass. Breath.*'

'Nice. Sounds like a coded wartime message on Radio London.'

'It's Japanese poetry. A haiku.'

'What good is that to ku? I mean you?'

'It's good for capturing the evanescence of things.'

He frowned.

'Evanescence,' I explained, 'means when things in life are about to vanish and you have to hold on to them.'

Napoleon started to wave his hand about in front of his face as if he had burnt himself. 'Give me an example of your eva-whatsit.'

I shut my eyes. I felt Napoleon's gaze upon me.

'OK, how about this? *A lonely suitcase. Football on the tiles. Everyone gone.*'

'Good, there aren't too many words. Can I try?'

He concentrated, took a deep breath and then recited in one go, '*A jab to the face. A nose pissing blood. K.O.*'

He watched my face for a reaction.

'Not bad!' I said. 'Not bad at all.'

A smile tinged with indescribable sadness spread across his fine features, a smile of the same softness as his white hair. Once more he walked away from me. Without a backward glance he rode off into the vast empty plains of old age, his horse's hooves drumming on the frozen ground.

'My emperor,' I whispered. 'My emperor . . . '

I heard a key turn in the lock.

'Josephine!' Napoleon cried. 'What took you so long?'

My heart was racing. But, no – it was the woman my father had employed. He pointed to me with his right hand.

'Thanks to this gentleman we've found the home of our dreams. Come, I'll show you around. We shall grow old together in this house and we shall never leave it. Josephine?'

'Yes, Napoleon,' the woman replied.

'I still have sand between my toes.'

A letter to Grandma

Grandma,

I'm writing to tell you about something terrible that happened last week. Sit down before you carry on reading, and put down your knitting for a bit. Even if you've finished it, undo a dozen rows because we still need you. I promised Napoleon that I'd never tell anyone, but I'm going to tell you because Napoleon is no longer Napoleon. He's so thin and wrinkled that he looks like an unironed sheet. You know, he's even losing whole handfuls of his beautiful white hair. You can see the top of his skull. At some moments it's as if he's left our world and he doesn't recognise anyone. Mum calls it the Venice of life, because it's like floating out of time, getting lost in a beautiful, shifting labyrinth. Other times, but less and less often, he still acts imperiously with all his anger intact and you wouldn't think he's changed at all. He still laughs a lot. His laughter fills the corridors and is so loud that the other day it set off the burglar alarm. I think that laughter might be the last thing to go.

And now I've completely understood about the divorce and his fresh start. He wanted to continue to be our emperor for ever and didn't want you to see him in this state and, most of all, not to see him in the big home where he is now with all the other people who don't fit the criteria for normal life.

You read that correctly. He agreed to leave the old house where he'd always lived with you. Where he's living now, there's just about enough room for a transistor radio, so he can listen to Who Wants To Win A Thousand Euros? and for the picture of Rocky, which he's hung directly opposite his bed. Sometimes I think he feels as if Rocky is his only family. It seems like Rocky is trying to reassure him by saying, 'Come on, come on, don't be scared, you'll see that things'll be just fine when the two of us are together.'

The home provides everything apart from batteries for the remote control for the television, and that doesn't matter because he doesn't watch TV anyway. He says it's for old people. See, he's still fighting.

They've given him a room on the second floor with a view of the school playground. He can see me, and I can see him too. Twice a week he comes into my classroom and sits next to me. I'm sure you'll be glad to hear that he's a good pupil who pays attention. He speaks in a way you wouldn't understand. He mixes up all the letters and you have to fish them out and rearrange them to understand him, so often he talks with his eyes.

We keep an eye on each other, see. Maybe one day, after watching out for each other for so long, we'll do a bunk, the two of us, do a massive bunk without looking back. That's my dream, but I know he'll run off on his own. I didn't use to believe it was possible, but now I do. That's why you have to be ready when he decides that he wants to see you again, because there won't be much time left. He'll be glad to know you've knitted him a jumper. Don't be angry if he doesn't write to you. One day I'll explain why.

Lots of love,

Leonard

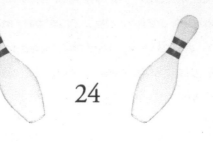

24

A few weeks passed.

During break Alexandre and I would keep an eye out for Napoleon's appearance at his window. He'd give us a little wave. His face had become as sharp as a knife blade and his gaze as wavering as a candle flame. He would stick out a clenched fist, and we made the same gesture back.

We admired him.

He smiled from behind the glass. Even locked up, even if his empire had dwindled away to next to nothing, he was still the pirate he'd always been, and there was still the same undimmed glint of rebellion in his eye.

'Yeah, he organises boxing matches in the hallways and bowling contests!'

'Ooh!'

'He trains a team of backing dancers until two in the morning! And . . . and . . . '

'And?'

'And he rebels! He couldn't give a damn!'

'Nor could I!' Alexandre cried.

'Me neither,' I echoed.

'Oh, that was excellent! Here, have a marble! Take one!'

Napoleon caused such unholy chaos in the care home that my parents were summoned by the director.

'Playing "Alexandrie Alexandra" and "Le mal aimé" until two in the morning was bad enough.'

'We did warn you,' my father said.

'Wait, I haven't finished. I've no problem with imagination.' She paused for a second, folded her hands together and continued, 'Most of his behaviour is, um, borderline. But today all the boundaries have been over-overstepped and I say no. No, no, no! After all, rules are there to be observed. Norms, if you prefer.'

'I agree. Rules aren't necessarily his strong suit,' my father said.

It turns out that Napoleon and several of his burly friends had locked the lifeguard in the swimming pool changing rooms.

'After stealing his trunks,' the director added. 'We've had to put the lifeguard on sick leave. But that was just the beginning, merely for starters. Napoleon encouraged the other residents to nick tomatoes from the dining hall … Do you know why?'

My parents and I shook our heads.

'To throw at the poor accordion player who comes to entertain them every Wednesday. The residents have enjoyed his nice music for twenty years, then your father gets here and they turn on the accordion player and he gets pelted with tomatoes. They hit him right on the nose!'

'It's true that accordions can seriously get on your nerves,' said my father.

'They're clamouring for pop and reggae. Dance music! Everyone's demanding double rooms and Bob Marley posters. They want to smoke marijuana. No, it's no use – your father is beyond the pale. He's the instigator, the guru, the ringleader!'

'The emperor!' my father muttered.

'Emperor, if you like. In fact, that's what his friends call him. Or admiral, when they go to the pool.'

So Napoleon was writing the final pages of his book with lines of fire. In less than a month at the peaceful 'welcome home' he had sown the seeds of rebellion, a legacy that would be remembered long after he had left this earth.

The day after this conversation, my father laid down the law to my grandfather at the director's behest.

'They geiv tomeny odders in this hoem,' was all Napoleon could be bothered to say. 'And I doent liek odders.'

'Too many orders?' my father stammered. 'What about

the lifeguard you imprisoned, was he giving you too many orders as well?'

'I dint let misell be deorpted to waev my arms in the watre.'

'Firstly,' my father exclaimed, 'stop saying you've been deported. Secondly, waving your arms around in the water is good for your health. He was getting you to do exercises for your own wellbeing. YOUR OWN WELLBEING.'

Napoleon shrugged his shoulders. 'Doen shout liek that, Im not def.'

'I'm not shouting, I'm explaining!'

'His littel loepardskin strunk wer getting on my ncervs.'

'What have leopard-skin trunks got to do with this?'

A crafty smile suddenly lit up my grandfather's face. He signalled with his forefinger for my father to come closer and whispered into his ear. My father listened and then suddenly recoiled, clearly shocked.

'What's that? He had a tiny ... Good grief, Dad, you've gone totally bonkers! Seriously, I'll never understand you.'

'I knwo. Weve vener unsterdood each othre. An dyet ... '

'An dyet ... I mean, and yet what?' my father asked, pulling himself up onto his tiptoes.

'And yet nothing. Turn on the radio, it's time for *Who Wants To Win A Thousand Euros?*'

The three silvery notes signalled the daily truce. *Ding-ding-ding.* For an hour everything would return to normal.

A letter from Grandma

My darling boy,

I haven't stopped knitting since I received your
latest letter. No matter if I have blisters on my
hands, a blister on your hand is only dangerous if
you're Cloclo (sorry, that's a stupid joke, I'm the
one blowing a fuse). I'd knit with my feet if I could,
day, night, morning and evening, I think only of
the day when Napoleon wants me by his side and
I'll be able to give him his jumper. At least he'll be
nice and warm in the Venice of his life where it's so
unbelievably damp.

   If he does leave without saying goodbye, tell him
it doesn't matter and that I thought of him every
minute of my life and every minute of his death I'll
think of him, and also that my only regret is not to
have been able to return to that beach. I can't even
remember how old we were, I could work it out but
I'm scared to. I can't stop looking at the map to
make sure that it really does exist, I don't know why,

but he and I never went back there when it was all still possible, it's stupid, you need to do things when they're possible, that's the only lesson you need to learn, everything else you can throw in the bin.

You know, I never took his fresh start as targeting me; it's a pride thing, men get an urge to live when they think of death, death is the only thing Napoleon was afraid of. At night before I go to sleep, I sometimes think that I should have stuck by him and never left that house, but I also tell myself that leaving was like a gift I gave him, that I have kept in my eyes and my heart the fine image he wishes to leave behind so that he can remain Napoleon. Perhaps you haven't experienced this yet, but humans are incredibly complicated.

Speaking of complicated, just imagine this: Edouard has found a high-class life assistant who knows a lot about Eastern things. He's hardly in touch now. He called me the other night to tell me that he couldn't see me this week because of a never-ending game of Go. His assistant is a pro. Apparently, they went to see *Seven Samurai* again together twice. It seems that his poor assistant has had some very bad times professionally, they go well together and he suggested that he was planning to adopt her. He told me over the phone, 'Can you believe it? I'm going to be a father, at my age!'; when I told Edouard I'd gone back to my knitting, he told me that there was no hurry because he was going off to Japan with his assistant or his daughter, I don't know what to call her any more, on a cruise and for a tour of the Noh theatres. There was a long silence on the line, he was very embarrassed. I didn't have the courage to tell him that the reason I was hurrying had nothing to do with him, and in an emotional and very affectionate voice he added that he had almost become besotted with me. I nearly started crying, but I no longer knew why. I simply replied, 'Happiness is being with your Sunshine!'

Writing letters is like knitting, I cannot stop, but now I have to go back to my needles.

Big hugs and kisses

25

A ritual was established. Twice a week, after morning break, Napoleon came and sat in class with two or three of his friends, whom he'd managed to persuade to tag along on this final campaign. Each of them had a little exercise book with his name on it. Alexandre and I formed a guard of honour for them, inviting derision from our classmates, but we felt untouchable. No one was going to steal our dream from us.

One day Napoleon stopped in front of Alexandre and looked him up and down, from his strange cap to his worn-out trainers.

'This is Private Rawcziik,' I whispered.

'You have fought valiantly, Private Raw—, um . . . Raw-whatever. I name you lieutenant general. My pal will need a helping hand when the emperor is gone.'

My desk would have been wide enough for the two of us if Napoleon hadn't insisted on sticking his elbows out. I gladly forgave him the smudges and crossings-out I made when he knocked his elbow against mine. After all, this was only true to form: he continued to take up a great deal of room.

Napoleon's friends were also bent on making up for a particular period of their lives when they felt they'd missed out on something. Each of them had a Madame Taillandec with whom they wanted to settle some old scores. One man had never learned to do long division properly, another couldn't tell a rhombus from a rectangle and the third had never been able to get his head around verb conjugations. None of them understood why the world was in such a sorry state, and neither they nor our teacher nor Victor Hugo, hanging in his glass frame above the blackboard, had ever found a satisfactory answer to that question.

During these last few weeks the enemy seemed to retreat, as if he didn't dare step through the school gates.

'He was on top form today!' cried Alexandre.

I pretended to believe him. How delightful it can sometimes be to ignore reality! Napoleon followed the textbook with great concentration, tracing the sentences with his finger. We rode the words as if on a slide – a slide he and I would surely have skittered down together if we'd been the same age at the same time.

I left Alexandre immediately after school that evening, as I sometimes did, in order to visit Napoleon in his little room.

My grandfather was particularly reserved and continued to file away at his nails (a habit from his boxing days to avoid breaking them with a punch).

'Grandpa, you see Rocky over there.'

He raised his eyes to the picture, and a smile lit up his face.

'He's still there,' I continued. 'You've kept his memory alive; we think of him every day. He still has pride of place. You don't truly disappear as long as people go on thinking about you. It's when there's no one left to remember you that you're truly gone, but as long as there's someone, then it isn't over yet. The only enemy is forgetting, don't you think?'

'Ah, that Rocky certainly made his mark. There's no way he'll ever be forgotten. He had the knack. A crafty fellow he was! Stronger than all of us put together.' Keeping his eyes on the photo, he raised his hand to his forehead in salute. 'I salute you. Bravo! You know what, pal?'

'No, but I'm listening.'

'It isn't hard to identify the main purpose of life. Enjoy yourself with people you like. Forget the rest – it's not important. Will you remember how much fun we've had? We've had a laugh, haven't we? Tell me we've had a laugh. It makes me feel good.'

'Yes, my emperor, we've had a laugh. No one has ever had as big a laugh as we have.'

'In the future you'll pass on a very simple message to those around you: "I had a grandfather and we had fun together." They'll understand.'

'Yes, I'll say that. I won't forget. *I had a grandfather and we had fun together.* I'll try to remember.'

'Want me to write it down for you?'

He smiled and his grin stretched the entire width of his face.

'Can you?' I asked.

'Almost. I used to have all kinds of trouble, but sitting next to you it sank in automatically. I must've been able to write once, but then I forgot.'

I handed him my exercise book. He wetted the tip of his pen by pressing it against his tongue and, taking care not to go beyond the lines, began to form letters.

'There you are. Now you'll never forget.'

I had a grand fatha and we had funn to getha.

A short silence. There was a lump in my throat. I just about mustered the strength to say, 'And we're going to have some more laughs, right?'

'Sure. You'll see some fun very soon.'

What did he mean by that? What kind of fun was he talking about? A shiver ran the whole length of my spine.

All of a sudden, an embarrassed look stole over his face. 'I've a favour to ask,' he mumbled.

He reached under his pillow and pulled out a page from a notebook folded into four. He held it out, but just as I was

236

about to take it he jerked back his hand and said in a suspicious tone of voice, 'You won't make fun of your emperor?'

'Of course not.'

'Promise?'

'I promise.'

'OK, you can take it. I wrote it myself. Letters come in pretty handy, actually. There may be some mistakes, but nothing serious – you can correct them. Add some commas and full stops – I'll make a note of the punctuation separately. Hurry up, though, because it's pretty urgent. Send it first class and remember that this isn't a . . . '

'Surrender . . . Merely a decoy tactic.'

'Correct. You're the only person who understands me.'

'Me and Rocky.'

'You and Rocky.'

Totally focused on my mission, I ran home through empty streets bathed in sunshine. The world was one huge hourglass with time pouring through it. I reckoned that with a bit of luck the letter would go off the very next morning. Every second was precious.

Our front door was ajar. I pushed it open with a sudden certainty that I'd stumble upon some terrible scene on the other side. My footsteps echoed in the empty hallway. My mother's handbag had been abandoned on the table, and the keys were lying on the floor tiles. My heart was hammering. I froze at the sound of a cry from the living room.

Alexandre was standing in front of my mother, who was seated and dabbing his face with a ball of cotton wool soaked with iodine.

'I look a complete clown, right?' Alexandre said. He was smiling through the pain, and his nose was still bleeding slightly.

'They saw I was alone, so they followed me.' He laughed a little. 'But I put up a fight. I saved Napoleon's marbles and my cap.' He raised it like someone doffing their hat, back in the olden days.

'Stand still,' my mother whispered, 'or I won't be able to clean it.'

Alexandre immediately did so. Legs braced, he whispered, 'I promise I'll never move again.'

I held my breath so as not to burst this little bubble of trust.

A flood of questions overwhelmed all my other thoughts. Why was my mother there when he was attacked? Did she chase the boys away? Or did he come here of his own accord because he didn't know where else to go for help?

She put away the plasters and bandages and closed the little bottle of iodine. Then she took Alexandre's hands and inspected each palm in turn – tiny flecks of paint mixing shades of green, blue and yellow. She let out a peal of laughter, and Alexandre joined in with her.

'Have you used them all up already?' my mother asked.

'Yes,' Alexandre replied.

'I got through paints like nobody's business at your age too. I'll give you some more next time.'

'Lots of different colours?'

'Lots.'

My curiosity gradually gave way to a happiness at seeing the two of them together. I chose to keep silent, because what I liked about them were the things they'd never say.

A letter from Napoleon

Before

Its all ova wiv mi fresh stat dea Josefin
Im soree I dee vorsed yu and kikced u
out it was all becos of my feer a bout the
larst fite I thort that geting old ment
just not giv ing up But it duz ent werk
like that The o po nent
   is 2 strong, much 2 strong and the ref
was bribd You woent beleev this but I hav
no strenth lefd in mi fist no reech nuffin but
jellee in mi legs, powda puf punchs I fort
for as long as I cood but I hav no mor
desire I wont lars much longa I carnt stan
dup and done speek much I even losd mose
of my luvli hare no matta tho cos I can
feel yor hand runing thru it and my toof is
gone but Id be sprized if the toof fe ree
caim funee that, 2 teef left the onlee fing

240

I stil wan

 is to cee u and spen the rest of mi life
wiv u If u cum u mite micks mi up wiv the
sheet I am under neef try 2 pre tend
that yor not sprized an al so therz that
fing own lee u no a bout

 u no wat I meen

 I neva won ted to oen up but I doen
wan 2 go 2 meat Ro Ki wiv out tellin
the truthe.

 Napoleon

```
.............  )))))))))
............ ))))))))  )))))))
!!!!!!!!
```

Ad this punk
chuayshun,
mate

After

It's all over with my fresh start, dear Josephine. I'm sorry I divorced
you and kicked you out. It was all because of my fear of the last
fight; I thought that getting old meant just not giving up, but
it doesn't work like that. The opponent is too strong, much too
strong and the ref was bribed. You won't believe this, but I have
no strength left in my fists, no reach, nothing in my legs, powder-
puff punches. I've fought for as long as I could, but I have no more
desire. I won't last much longer. I can't stand up and I don't speak

much. I've even lost most of my lovely hair, but it doesn't matter because I can feel your hand running through it. And my teeth are almost gone, but I'd be surprised if the tooth fairy came. Only two teeth left. The only thing I still want is to see you and spend the rest of my life with you. If you do come, you might mix me up with the sheet; I'm underneath it. Try to pretend you're not surprised.

And also there's that thing only you know about. You know what I mean. I never wanted to own up, but I don't want to go to meet Rocky without telling the truth.

Napoleon

I posted the letter at dawn the next day. And waited.

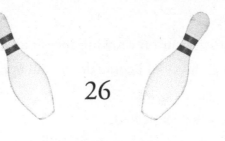

26

The next night I was struck down with an inexplicable fever, which confined me to bed. It came as a blessing to me. I spent hours lying in my bed with my hands behind my head, my mind numb. I wondered about the secret Napoleon had mentioned in his letter, the one that was weighing so heavily on his mind. How would I react if I were to learn that he'd never been a boxer and had lied to me all my life? For one crazy instant I even began to hope he might leave with his secret intact, like a gold-laden Spanish galleon that had sunk with all hands, inspiring fantasies down through the centuries.

I would occasionally drift off to sleep, and the trees would begin to fall again, on and on, like obedient soldiers. When I awoke, my bedclothes were drenched with sweat. Rain was battering the roof. Endov wandered in and out of my room but even Napoleon's faithful companion couldn't offer me much comfort. The hours passed slowly, sticky and hopeless.

My mother went on drawing incessantly upstairs. From time to time she would come down and open my door. My eyes met hers.

'Are you OK?' she asked.

'I'll feel better soon,' I replied. 'What are you doing?'

She held up her paint-covered hands. 'I have to hurry,' she murmured.

Alexandre rang the doorbell in the late afternoon. Endov seemed melancholy and was wrapping himself around my legs. I realised that I'd been waiting for Alexandre to arrive.

'Your turn to tell me about today,' I told him.

'He didn't show up.'

'All day?'

'All day. And no one came to the window either. Were you expecting this?'

I nodded.

He smiled, adding, 'He's no longer at his window, but he will always look down on us.' He lowered his gaze and untied the little bag hanging from his belt. 'Here,' he said. 'There are only two left. Take them.'

I grabbed them and opened my hand in front of my eyes. The two marbles rested on my cupped palm.

'One each,' I said.

'Napoleon's legacy,' Alexandre whispered. 'An inheritance has to be divided between brothers.'

I held the marble Alexandre had given me between my thumb and index finger and raised it to the light.

'Beautiful, isn't it?' he said.

'Yes,' I murmured. 'It sparkles. You get the feeling it has all kinds of things trapped inside it.'

'Secret things.'

'Every time I look at it I'll think of you,' I said.

'Whenever we meet up, we'll have this sign. Even if that only happens many years from now, we'll recognise each other, and the marbles will shine as brightly as they do now.'

His cap was dangling from one hand, and I couldn't look away. Our eyes met, and there was a glint in his.

He whispered, 'I'm going to be able to return it to my father. He gets out of prison today. We're going to be together again. I want to show you what he looks like.'

'Do you have a photo?'

'Better than that – much better. Look.'

The portrait was breathtaking and simple. I recognised my mother's customary thick paper and colour scheme.

'We're never very far from those we love,' he said. 'Even when we're apart.'

As he carefully stowed the drawing in his schoolbag, I said quietly, 'She really taught you how to draw.'

'What she really taught me was hope. Hope and joy. Let her know that, OK?'

I nodded and touched his cap for the last time.

'So this is his cap?' I asked.

'Yes. R for Raphael. But it doesn't only belong to him: it belongs to my whole family, starting with my great-grandfather and then my grandfather, who handed it down to my father.'

'And eventually it'll be yours.'

He nodded. 'It's travelled a lot. We keep it as a memento. That's why we must never lose it.'

'A memento of what?'

'A memento of journeys from which no one ever returns.'

And with that he rushed out without even bothering to shut the door.

I spent another night with the fallen trees. I was now alone among them, without Alexandre or even Endov for company in my dreams. I was awoken mid-morning by the sound of my dad's car engine. My mind was clear and my fever was gone. Why had my father come home at this time of day? I heard my mother's hurried footsteps on the stairs. The front door slammed and the car immediately pulled away, tyres crunching on the gravel. Then there was silence.

I replayed the images of Alexandre's visit in my mind. I felt very alone until I realised that my mother had slid some new drawings under my bedroom door before she left.

It was the end of Napoleon's book. There he was, sitting next to me in the classroom. His face at the window. The window without his face. I hardly recognised myself in these drawings. I looked far older than I was. The colours became increasingly pale as I approached the final page.

The final page was still empty. Blank.

Without thinking, I got out of bed. It was still raining, coming down in such torrents that wide, deep puddles had formed on the road. Cars had to slow down to manoeuvre through the street. The sky and the trees were spinning around me. I started to race at full tilt, but, as in a nightmare, I felt as if I were running on the spot. I sprinted headlong, my ears buzzing, as if this sprint might alter the course of events. The irreversible course of events. The rain was streaming down my face. The key in the lock.

Napoleon's house was deserted. Empty. Freezing. Most of the furniture had disappeared. Had my parents sold it? Where had it been scattered? The garden looked like a patch of jungle. I felt like going out and losing myself there. Then, all of a sudden, it appeared – a doe! Like the one my father had almost hit on our way back from the service station. It was there on the other side of the window, a matter of yards away. The garden's dense foliage set off its dazzling whiteness to startling effect. It froze, its head pointing straight at me. I tumbled into its soft, dark eyes. A few seconds later it was gone, so suddenly that I wondered if I hadn't been dreaming all along.

There was a light, rectangular patch on the wallpaper in the toilet where the portrait of Rocky had been.

I called, 'Napoleon? My emperor?'

The walls swallowed my voice. It was this silence that I would now have to face, this emptiness I would have to get used to. And yet Alexandre's words – 'We're never very far from those we love. Even when we're apart' – chased away my despondency.

The garage was clean and no longer in its usual untidy state. The only things that remained were Napoleon's old boxing gloves, tied together by the laces. The smell of the leather was still the same, and the inside still gave off the familiar whiff of victorious sweat. I put them around my neck.

The rain continued to fall. The sky was overcast, the clouds hanging low. I set out along the dirt track that connected the house to the main street of our town.

A sturdy tree with rough bark, an oak that had appeared indestructible, blocked the drive. Its roots had been torn from the waterlogged soil. Thousands of insects were now converging in orderly columns on this new shelter. I retreated a couple of paces, setting my feet down with great care. Don't crush anything. Stepping forward, I ran my hands over the bark, lay down on the trunk and gazed up into the sky. It was grey, uniform and motionless, as mysterious as life itself.

A few minutes passed, or perhaps a few hours.

I ran towards my grandfather, and in the unrelenting rain I couldn't be sure whether I was laughing or weeping.

27

Josephine was there, opposite Napoleon's bed. She greeted me with a wordless smile. She vanished into the bathroom and reappeared within seconds with a white towel she used to dry my hair. I still felt so feverish.

Napoleon looked well rested. Younger almost. Swamped by Josephine's jumper, he lay with his arms by his sides, fists clenched.

'I'm sorry to disappoint you if you've come for an arm-wrestle,' he mumbled weakly when he caught sight of me.

I saw that they'd connected him to a machine whose screen showed a steady stream of numbers.

'See, pal?' he sighed. 'You can never escape from the meter! It'll have the last word after all. Try not to let the meters catch up with you. Nor square-toed shoes!' He flashed my father an affectionate smile, adding, 'Don't you start blubbering, lad!'

'I'll blub if I want to!' my father replied.

Napoleon turned to me. 'Is it time?'

I nodded and switched on the little transistor radio. What's-his-face's, the presenter's, reassuring voice filled the room. The contestant was a recently retired judge, and, as was What's-his-face's wont when he welcomed someone with a slightly unusual profession, he asked the man for his most striking memory.

'I've seen some extraordinary cases during my long career as a judge, but, believe me, my finest memory is of a former boxer, an eighty-five-year-old maniac, who got divorced to embark on a new life. Believe me, I thought I'd met an immortal that day!'

Napoleon nodded off halfway through the super jackpot. I turned off the radio before the programme finished. The silence was oppressive, broken only by the electronic beeping of the machine.

'You should leave the room,' my father began. 'This isn't—'

'No, you three should leave.' It was Napoleon. His voice was feeble, virtually inaudible. 'I have some instructions for my pal about the future governance of the empire. Go and get some coffee. Don't worry, I'll still be alive when you get back.'

No one chuckled along with him at this comment but, as usual, they couldn't deny his request. Once they were gone, I moved closer, my ear to his lips.

'First of all, pal, unplug this damn meter. There's not much left to measure.'

The machine fell abruptly silent.

'No time to get emotional, pal. Let's deal with our most pressing business. First, from now on you are not my general – I'm handing over supreme command of the empire to you. Do with it what you will.'

'I'll take good care of it. You can go in peace.'

'Next, I'd like you to know that I've fought to the bitter end, but there was nothing I could do. The enemy's stronger in every respect.'

The gloves. His fists slipped inside them with ease. I pulled the laces tight.

'Keeping boxing up above. Punch as hard as you can. At the beginning, in the middle and ... at the end.' He flashed me a smile. 'My old pal,' he said, 'you're going to have to work this out for yourself, because I'm not sure I can put it into words.' He raised a fist and gazed straight ahead at Rocky's portrait.

My eyes met his once more. Was ... ? No, there was obviously something I didn't get. Or else I wasn't fully awake. Or my fever was returning ... But I thought back to Napoleon's birthday, the scene in the kitchen, and above all to my mother's drawing of it. The gloves. The worn gloves. Rocky's ... and my father's ...

My heart skipped a beat. I could hardly breathe. I held my hand up to my mouth to stop myself from screaming. I moved even closer to Napoleon.

'Have you figured it out?' he whispered so quietly that I could barely hear what he said.

'I think so.'

'Nice trick, eh?'

'But it's so . . .'

'A masterpiece, I know.'

'That match wasn't rigged, was it?'

'Yes, it was, but I rigged it. I wasn't lying. Come closer and listen. Between rounds Rocky told me he was sick. He was sick and only had a few weeks to live. Some horrible thing eating him up from the inside. A boxer never lies, particularly Rocky. I knew him well, and I could see in his eyes that he was telling the truth. I could see the sadness of a man about to hang up his gloves. That was when he asked me . . .'

'To let him win. He begged you to let him go out on a high.'

'No . . . That was my idea. My natural generosity. He had a little boy with him, a tiny little boy. A little shrimp. I don't know why the boy's mother wasn't there. We boxers lead strange lives, you know. He asked me to take care of him. To raise him and pass on his gloves and make a truly great boxer out of him. To make him a champion in memory of Rocky – a champion who would achieve what he hadn't had time to accomplish. He was sure the boy would take after him. Most importantly, he asked me never to tell the boy who his father was. But, as you can see, I could only keep half of my promise. I failed with the rest. Rocky will haul me over the coals a few hours from now.'

'No, you didn't fail. You're the emperor and your reign shall never end.'

'You may be right. Perhaps where I failed was in not getting to know him properly. That was so stupid of me!'

We were silent for a while. I was shocked. And then, just like that, everyone came back into the room.

'What did he say?' my father whispered.

'Oh, nothing. That you were the best son ever, Dad. And also . . .'

Through my tears I cast my eyes over the others, who were hanging on my every word. 'And also that he'd like to . . .'

But the word wouldn't come out. They all saw the gloves on Napoleon's small hands. My father was leaning against the wall a couple of feet from Napoleon and Rocky's picture. I wondered if he'd known all along. My grandfather turned to Josephine and their eyes met, shining with intensity.

My words still wouldn't come out. Josephine closed her eyes. It was impossible. My mother conjured up a drawing from the page.

The beach. The final page.

Pursued by the director, we raced along the corridors past the other residents, who had emerged from their rooms to salute the man who'd given them a new lease of life in recent weeks. We were pushing Napoleon in his wheelchair, and dozens of hands reached out to touch him, as they used to when he stepped out of the ring. Endov ran behind us.

'Stop right there!' the director called out. 'Stop this! You've over-overstepped the mark again; there are documents to sign, waivers to fill out, permits to grant. Dogs are not allowed. This breaks every rule!'

To which my father offered the age-old retort, 'You know where you can stick your rules!'

I reckoned that there would at least be two of us to keep watch over the empire. Napoleon briefly emerged from his daze to cast an admiring glance at my father, who was electrified by this, and spun round to face the crowd in the corridor and shouted at the top of his lungs, 'HE'S MY FATHER!'

The director was on the phone in her glass-walled office by this stage.

My father frantically set the satnav in his powerful car. The route appeared on the screen and the electronic voice announced, 'Go for it!'

I was certain that it was none other than Rocky speaking. The engine thrummed. My father was in the front, with Napoleon propped up between Josephine and me, and Endov at our feet. We sank into the leather seats.

'How long have we got, Dad?' my father shouted in an unfamiliar tone of voice.

Slipping in and out of consciousness, Napoleon stammered, 'No idea, lad. Not long. If you're going to lose your licence, then today's the day.' Within the first hundred and fifty miles on the motorway, his prediction came true. Flash, flash, flash: nine points up in smoke.

I whispered to Napoleon, 'See how famous you are? They can't stop taking photos of you.'

I couldn't tell if he had heard me. Josephine didn't say a word. She merely clasped Napoleon's glove to her chest and stared out at the passing scenery, her breath forming a circle of condensation on the window. Napoleon's head rocked gently back and forth before nestling against Josephine's neck. He looked like a child.

My father suddenly swerved into a service station to fill up with petrol. He searched for his wallet, rummaging in all his pockets, but finally had to face the facts.

'Shit, I left it at home.' He thought for a while. 'Damn. Too bad, who cares – I'm going to fill up anyway.'

I went to the counter with him. He explained the situation, gesticulating desperately. His chin was tense. His eyes filled with tears. He resembled a madman. They were going to have to call the manager. That would take too long, far too long. The conversation became heated. My dad found a few coins in the bottom of one of his pockets and slid them into a coffee machine, which served up a cup of dishwater. Two big punches in the side of the machine and it was jackpot time – two security guards.

'Causing trouble, are we? Hey, don't I know you? I've seen you before. Wet blankets, remember? Do you have a problem with coffee machines?'

Pow, pow – it was automatic. He floored one guard with a straight right that came from way back, deep down, from the very banks of the Hudson. One wet blanket down. The second retreated while my father stared at his fist as if he'd never noticed it before. He grabbed my hand and we walked to the car. The guard who was still standing yelled something into his radio. It was better if we didn't hang around.

We continued our journey. We were outlaws now. The mood was heavy with silent pain, and Napoleon was a shadow of himself. He barely had enough strength to stammer, 'I saw your jab back there at the service station. It was champion!'

'Thanks, Dad,' my father shouted.

'But watch your footwork.'

Napoleon turned to me with a superhuman effort. His mouth opened and shut several times before his reedy voice said, 'We'll stay in touch, pal.'

Telling myself that these might well be the last words he would ever say to me, I replied, 'We'll stay in touch.'

My father was silent. Time passed and we were five butterflies sailing into a great net.

We reached the toll booth, and there were indeed three police cars blocking our path. My father slowed down.

'We're screwed,' he said.

Napoleon was going to pass away surrounded by cops at a toll-booth barrier. Maybe all alone, while we were arrested.

My father murmured, 'I'm sorry, Dad. I'd have loved to make you happy one last time.'

He got out and tried to explain, but two police officers immediately slammed him down on the bonnet, with one arm twisted behind his back. Another man, who appeared to be the commanding officer, approached and walked around the car. My mother rolled down her window.

'We're on our way to the beach,' she said simply.

'To the beach? You must be pulling my leg. Well, your beach is going to be nice and shady and undisturbed. No need for any sun cream either.'

His eyes scanned the inside of the car, lingering on the baggy sweater with Napoleon somewhere inside it. His expression froze. His brow furrowed. The director of the old people's home must have reported that one of her residents was on the run. The police officer was mesmerised by the sight of the boxing gloves.

'Born to win,' he whispered.

Our eyes met.

'The 1951 title fight against Rocky?' he asked.

I smiled and said, '1952. A rigged bout.'

Turning to my father, who was still flat on the bonnet, in a loud, clear voice he asked, 'How much longer?'

'He's almost out for the count.'

Three minutes later the sirens were wailing. We followed two motorbikes driving at full speed to clear the road for us. The traffic stopped, cars pulled over to the hard shoulder, red lights turned green and the lamp posts bowed respectfully as we passed.

Napoleon opened his eyes and mumbled, 'Take that, Victor Hugo!'

Rocky's voice issued from the satnav again. 'You have reached your destination. Your journey is over.' Then, ten seconds later, it added, 'Good luck.'

The beach. The sun was falling into the sea. We walked towards the water, supporting Napoleon under his armpits. His feet dragged on the sand. He smiled. That smile was the only sign that he was still with us. I no longer felt like crying. Josephine carried his shoes.

We laid him down in the sand with his head on Josephine's lap. Endov rolled onto his side. There was nothing to do but wait and listen to the waves. Surf broke gently on the beach. A few yards away, the rising tide swept away a sandcastle built by a child. At the far end of the beach, a couple were holding hands as they walked along, leaving imprints on the sand.

Napoleon just about managed to mumble something, his words mingling with the sound of the waves.

My father waited a second before asking, 'What did he say?'

With a smile I replied, 'He says this is a beautiful place to die.'

Epilogue

The months passed. We broke up for the summer and I left primary school for good. After the holidays, I started secondary school and began a new life, with Endov by my side.

One of the playground supervisors at school ran a variety of different clubs, and some weeks we saw him virtually every day. He ended up showing an interest in our extra-curricular activities, and one day I told him that I'd taken up boxing.

'But I'm far less talented than my grandpa,' I added.

Even as I spoke those words, I realised that I had no idea if I was talking about Napoleon or Rocky or both.

The supervisor pointed to a small scar that ran across his eyebrow. 'See this?'

'Yes.'

'Well, believe it or not, I ran into a boxer once. Just the

one, but that was more than enough. It was last year, damn it, and I'm still shaken up! Some friends and I used to hang out at the bowling alley and mess around. One day we were a bit pissed and we started heckling an old bloke who was on an incredible run of strikes. Not much, just some light banter ... '

'And?' I asked.

'Well, he didn't appreciate it. There were ten of us and he took us out one after the other.'

'No way!'

'Yes way. I swear, he must have been at least eighty and as thin as a rake. I'm telling you, he took us on one by one. Bang, bang, bang! We went down like ducks at a fairground shooting gallery. Hey, are you listening to me? Anyone at home?'

I could hear the pins crashing to the floor and the crowd applauding. Napoleon gave a deep bow like a circus ringmaster. And between my fingers I felt Alexandre's marble promising me my share of eternity.

Acknowledgements

I would like to express my warmest gratitude to Karine Hocine and the whole team at Éditions Jean-Claude Lattès for the enthusiasm with which they greeted this novel and how easy it was to work together.

About the Author

Pascal Ruter grew up in the southern suburbs of Paris. He is the author of several books for young readers. *The Last Adventure of Napoleon Sunshine* is his first work of adult fiction. Ruter loves stories above everything, especially ones where the misfortune and severity of life are matched by the absurdity and humour of everyday situations. He currently lives in a tiny village in the middle of the forest of Fontainebleau.